A DANGEROUS AFFAIR

Was Seth Paslew a smuggler? How else could one explain the fine clothes, the thoroughbred horse, the good wines and brandy. Probably those coming to the meeting tonight were smugglers too.

Then I heard them—the men of the moors. They came silently and secretly, one by one, in the dark. I crouched at the window, staring into the darkened yard below. They didn't bring their lanterns for fear of being seen. They spoke in low voices and entered the house.

I lay down on the bed, tense and afraid, a pulse beating in my head, praying for sleep that would not come. Then suddenly I heard a cat crying and got up to unbolt the door. As I tiptoed past the closed door of the meeting room I heard Seth Paslew's husky voice, "I think it would be best if we lie low for a while."

There were cries of dismay. Then Seth's angry voice shouted, "Would you all prefer to dance on the end of a rope?"

Then to my horror, the door started to open. I blew out the candle and pressed myself as hard as I could against the wall of the dark hallway . . .

HISTORICAL ROMANCE IN THE MAKING!

The HOUSE on the HEATH

BY MAUREEN STEPHENSON

ZEBRA BOOKS
KENSINGTON PUBLISHING CORP.

ZEBRA BOOKS
are published by
KENSINGTON PUBLISHING CORP.
475 Park Avenue South
New York, N.Y. 10016
Copyright © 1979 by Kensington Publishing Corp.

Second Printing

Printed in the United States of America

CHAPTER 1

After we left the village the road wound uphill all the way.

Somewhere overhead a lark was singing.

I had entered a world of dazzling white limestone. It was in the dry stone walls that marked the small irregular fields on the left. It protruded through the fells that rose beyond the fields. It was in the cliff that towered majestically out of a small valley on the right, cutting a sharp silhouette against the sky. It was a white and green world, for the grass was the richest green I had ever seen.

The old carrier sat beside me on the cart, dressed in an ancient bottle-green coat with patches at the elbow, and a battered felt hat pulled snugly over his head. Unshaven and unwashed, he clutched a clay pipe between yellowing teeth. The cart behind us was filled with yarn for the weavers; a canvas bag held a few pieces of mail.

"That's Wath Cliff," he said, following my gaze. "Last year a revenue man were thrown over there."

He spoke with a certain satisfaction, then puffed contentedly at his pipe.

"Who threw him over?" I asked indignantly.

"That's not for me to say," he replied, looking at me slyly with his bloodshot eyes. "Then there were this young feller last winter. Verdict were suicide." There was a note of disbelief in his voice. "We have our own laws up here," he continued, "for folks who go poking their nose into matters that don't concern them. Reckon you'll be finding that out for yourself afore long."

I did not speak much after that.

It was when he stopped the cart to deliver a letter to a wayside cottage that I thought of the letter I had sent to Leah. Why had she not answered it? I searched my mind for some explanation and could find none. At first I had thought she was ill; now I was not so sure. Perhaps she had not wished to answer it? But that was so unlike her— not the sister I remembered.

I remembered a gentle, kind girl, preferring daydreams to reality. Perhaps that was why she had eloped with Seth Paslew—because he fitted into her dreamworld.

We lived in a comfortable house at Calverley, just a few miles outside Leeds, in the West Riding of Yorkshire. Father owned the Calverley Iron Forge two miles downriver, near enough for his daily visit, and far enough away so that we could not hear the hammering and din, nor see the black smoke rising from the chimneys.

We had been educated, if you can call it that, at Mistress Bucktrout's Academy for Young Ladies, a newly established school for the daughters of the rising, prosperous middle classes. Mistress Bucktrout had taught us the bare essentials, and a little sewing and embroidery; my brother Jonathan had received an excellent education at Leeds Grammar School, and was now studying medicine in London at Bart's. This had been father's first disappointment, having always cherished the hope that Jonathan would one day become his partner at the forge. But Jonathan had been adamant. It was medicine or nothing, so father had given in.

After Leah and I left Mistress Bucktrout's our education continued, or shall I say really began. Our home was full of books, and we were encouraged to read them. Leah settled down to learn German, while I chose Italian. My mother was a very practical woman who taught us cooking and household management. Leah and I took our turns in the daily chore of bread making, but we liked the autumn best when the fruits were ripe, and we helped to bottle and preserve them and make wine. My mother believed that a woman who was too proud to do these things was a fool.

Then one day last summer mother and I visited a sick family of one of the iron workers. When we returned home, Leah, who had remained behind, said someone had called from the forge with a message for father. His name was Seth Paslew.

From that day a change took place in Leah. At first it was hardly perceptible, just a feeling that there was something she did not wish to share with me. I found her new attitude puzzling, because Leah and I had always been close, sharing each other's secrets.

She took to disappearing those summer evenings, leaving me to make excuses for her absence. I did not question her, for I guessed she was meeting Seth Paslew. Only a lover could bring such a glow of happiness to her eyes. But even then I had a sense of uneasiness, of apprehension for her.

One September evening I went up to my room earlier than usual, and to my surprise Leah was waiting for me, her face radiant.

"I've been waiting for you, Damaris, because I want you to be the first to know. Seth Paslew has asked me to marry him!"

I was touched she wanted me to be the first to share her happiness. It was like old times.

"And have you agreed?" I asked.

"Of course. I love him."

I felt afraid for her.

"He is the only man you have ever known," I commented gently. "What makes you so sure you love him?"

"I'm so happy just to be near him," she replied simply.

"Father will be very angry," I warned her.

"I'm afraid of that," she replied. "But tonight I shall have to be brave and ask for his permission. When he realizes how much we love each other he will not refuse."

I did not share her confidence.

It was at dinner that night that the storm broke. Mother burst into a wail of weeping.

"An iron worker! I shall never be able to hold up my head again. Oh, the plans I had for you, Leah. I wanted you to marry into one of the best Leeds families."

Father's face flushed with anger.

"You little simpleton." he stormed. "It's only your money he wants."

"It is not, father," she insisted bravely. "He loves me for myself alone."

"Love!"

Father spit the word out with contempt.

"Seth Paslew doesn't know the meaning of it. I've heard his talk at the forge. He's an ambitious man with thoughts above his station, but I never thought he had

plans to marry one of my daughters. And you, Leah, fell into the trap."

"No, father," she cried.

"This is my second disappointment with this family. I've worked hard these past twenty years. When I inherited the forge it was on the verge of bankruptcy, and I've built it up into one of the best in the West Riding. I thought Jonathan was going to follow in my footsteps, but no, he couldn't get to London fast enough. And now you, humiliating me by wanting to marry one of my iron workers! Well, I'll put a stop to this. I forbid this marriage. If you disobey me you will receive not one penny from me."

Father paced up and down the room, his fists clenched.

"This family has owned the Calverley Forge for over two hundred years. We have a name to uphold, and if you marry one of my workers, we'll be the laughing stock of the county. It's almost as bad as the time that Charlotte Thorpe ran off with the groom."

Leah ran upstairs and locked the door of her room. I couldn't blame her. I could hear the muffled sobs through the door. Her humiliating interview with father could not have been worse. I am a romantic, but I also realized the risk in such a union. The income from the forge gave us an easy life, free from financial cares. Life with Seth Paslew would be hard; there would be little money, and Leah would be faced with problems she had never coped with before.

In the late evening, Leah unlocked her door and I went in and tried to comfort her. She sat on her bed, her eyes swollen and red from weeping. But her mind was made up. Father's insults had only served to strengthen her determination to marry Seth Paslew.

10

The next day mother talked to Leah endlessly. "Some madness has possessed you, child. I have done my best to bring you up as a lady. I was hoping for a good marriage because you would have had a substantial dowry, which is always encouraging to gentlemen who are short of capital. I beg of you to think very hard. Your whole life is before you, and you are going to throw it away on a penniless, illiterate iron worker."

I do not think mother's words had the slightest effect on Leah. She did not appear to live in our world, but wandered about the house with a distant look in her eyes. She scarcely spoke. She had put up a barrier, and the old friendship had gone.

I knew something terrible was going to happen. There was such tension in the house. Mealtimes were the worst. Father glowering at the head of the table, his lips set in a tight line. Mother pale and strained, and Leah looking like a ghost. The silence was hardest to bear. It was the silence before the storm.

A few days later Leah did not come down for breakfast. I went up to see what had happened, thinking she was ill.

I opened the door. The room was empty. The bed had not been slept in, and there was a note pinned to the curtains flapping at the open window.

Leah had eloped with Seth Paslew!

I wanted to cry. I ran downstairs and broke the news to the family. It was a day I shall never forget. Mother wept and father stormed out of the house saying he would see that Seth Paslew never got another job in an iron forge in the county, and he never wanted to see Leah again.

A week later we received a letter from Leah informing us that they had gone to live at Wath Riding on Wath Moor. It was Seth Paslew's father's farm, and she hoped

11

we would forgive her. Father did not answer the letter. Similarly, he refused to answer the letters that followed, and finally they ceased to come.

It was a hard winter with roads impassable with deep snow. Then spring came, bringing warm, sunny days. I often thought of Leah, and wondered about her new life. She had been my closest friend through childhood and adolescence, and I missed her more than I thought possible.

One night I dreamed about her. It was a strange, disturbing dream. She was in trouble and needed me. I could hear her calling my name, "Damaris! Damaris!" The dream occurred again and again, and as time went by a feeling of anxiety grew within me. I had to see her.

One day in May I confided my troubles to mother. It was fortuitous that father had left that morning on a long business trip.

"I want to visit Leah," I told her. "I miss her so much. Please, let me go."

"You know your father is away. I cannot give permission."

"I'll be back before he returns. He need never know, mother."

"That is underhanded of you, Damaris."

But I could see she was favorably considering it by the way she pursed her lips.

"Please, may I go to see her?" I persisted. "I beg of you."

Then brother Jonathan, who was home for a short holiday, intervened.

"Leah's been punished enough. Let Damaris go, mother. I'll take full responsibility."

"Very well," said mother. "But Damaris cannot travel

unaccompanied, and I can't spare Bessie."

"I can see her to the coach," said Jonathan. "And I'll tell the driver to keep an eye on her." He looked at me laughingly.

"At Settle I could hire a hackney carriage," I suggested. "I couldn't possibly come to any harm."

"You're right, my dear," smiled mother. "I worry far too much about you."

I quickly wrote an enthusiastic letter to Leah telling her I was coming in a week's time, which would be the last Saturday in May, and hoping it would be convenient to her. It was dispatched express, and there was time for Leah to reply, but she did not.

The day of my departure dawned bright and sunny, and as I stepped into the gig, mother came hurrying down the steps, a worried expression on her usually calm face.

"I'm not happy about you going, Damaris. You know there has been no reply from Leah."

"I think she's ill, mother, which is even more reason for going."

She was silent for a moment, then she said: "Tell her I've forgiven her."

"I will, mother," I replied fervently, kissing her on the cheek.

"Take care of yourself, and come home as quickly as you can."

"Goodbye, mother."

I felt very happy as we trotted along the tree-lined lane to the coaching inn. Jonathan was in good spirits too, glad of the short respite from his studies. I was full of eager anticipation. A journey, with my much loved sister at the end of it, was just what my stale spirits needed.

"Leah must have been mad to marry that fellow

13

Paslew," commented Jonathan. "I once saw him at the forge. Too arrogant for my liking. Anyway, he isn't a gentleman; father was right to act as he did."

"You mustn't condemn a man because he isn't a gentleman," I replied. "He is an honest craftsman, and remember, he's Leah's husband."

The coach was very crowded, and I was wedged uncomfortably in a corner next to a large woman nursing a baby. As the coach set off there was something about the young man in the opposite corner that caught my attention. His brown cloth coat, trimmed with velvet and gold buttons, had a foreign appearance, and his features were refined and yet sensitive, but it was his eyes that I noticed. There was such sorrow in them.

The elderly gentleman opposite spoke to him.

"Excuse me, sir, but your face is familiar. I feel we have met before."

"That is unlikely," he replied. "For I have just arrived from America."

"America!" exclaimed the elderly gentleman. "Is that not a country full of Indian savages?"

"Not entirely," he replied, looking away through the window. I could see that the elderly gentleman was eager for further conversation, but at that moment the baby started to cry and any further efforts were frustrated.

It was a terrible journey, for the roads were very bad, and great was my relief when we finally reached Settle. I saw the American gentleman enter a fine-looking coach and drive away as the rest of us crowded into the King's Head.

Saturday being market day, the inn was packed with farmers and their families, and it took me a considerable time to find the innkeeper. I finally located him in a back parlor. He was a big, pot-bellied man who wore a white apron.

"I would like to hire a hackney carriage," I said, feeling a little nervous. How I wished Jonathan was with me.

"Sorry, ma'am. There ain't no hackney carriages in Settle. Where you making for?"

"Wath Riding on Wath Moor."

A shadow seemed to cross his face, and he started to move away as if he did not wish to continue the conversation.

"But what am I to do? How far is it from here?"

"It be all of ten miles."

"Could I hire a saddle horse?"

"Hired out the last just an hour since."

Then his face relaxed. He must have felt sorry for me, for he suddenly said: "Harry the carrier is going up that way. I'll ask him to give you a lift."

The road had now leveled out and we were on a flat plateau of moorland. The carrier's voice broke into my thoughts.

"I'd like to know what a respectable woman like you is doing going to Wath Riding?"

"I'm going to visit my sister," I answered, surprised and a little indignant at his remark. And then I recalled the look on the innkeeper's face at Settle. Had it been a look of fear?

I looked about me. How dramatically the scene had changed. Gone was the dazzling limestone and the luscious green of the grass. Instead, the dark somberness of the moor, for the heather was not yet in bloom, billowed and swelled for mile upon mile, as far as the eye could see, and the road curled across it like a ribbon to

15

the horizon. In the distance blue fells, lonely and remote, folded line upon line.

The old cart creaked along the road. What a desolate place! I could see no sign of human habitation. A few sheep and goats grazing on the sparse vegetation were the only signs of life. Ahead of us by the roadside was a solitary tree, bent and misshapen by the winds of centuries.

It started to rain, and I gathered my cloak around me and pulled the hood down over my forehead. The bleak loneliness of the scene chilled me. And what of my sister Leah? Sweet, gentle Leah, who had made her home up here?

Suddenly the feeling of pleasurable anticipation I had felt all day vanished.

"How much further to Wath Riding?" I asked, making an effort to sound cheerful.

"Not more than a bit," the old man answered.

Suddenly the road dipped into a hollow and a farmhouse came into view.

"That's Wath Riding," said the carrier, pointing with his whip.

It was a solidly built stone farmhouse, like many in these parts, set back several hundred yards from the road and reached by a rough, muddy track. The windows were small and stone-mullioned. There was a porch with an arched Tudor entrance, and over the porch was a small, circular window. Patches of lichen clung to the stone-slated roof, and about a half mile beyond the farm, I caught the silver gleam of a small lake.

The cart lurched down into the hollow and stopped where the rough track began.

"This is as far as I go," the carrier said.

I looked with dismay at the mud I had to traverse to reach the gate, for I was wearing the thinnest of slippers. I climbed down from the cart, and the carrier handed me my baggage.

"I'm very grateful to you," I said, handing him a few coins. He seemed to be in a hurry to leave, for he quickly turned the cart around, gave the horse a flick of the whip, and set off.

In a few minutes I was alone, save for a pair of grouse who rose from the moor uttering that strange cry of theirs. Flapping their wings southward, they too soon disappeared from sight.

I picked up my baggage and set off along the track, jumping over the large puddles as best I could. The light was now fading from the sky, changing the clouds to the color of slate, and the horizon was pale turquoise.

Soon it would be dark.

As I approached the house I had the feeling that unseen eyes were watching me. I had rarely felt so ill-at-ease.

I reached the gate, and, putting my baggage down, I untied the rope that held it. It was difficult to open, being heavy and hanging on one hinge. In the forecourt before the house no flowers grew, and, carved over the porch, was the date *1601*, and the initials *S P & E C*.

Why was Leah not here to greet me?

Suddenly a black and white collie bounded up, nearly knocking me over. He jumped at me, barking, placing his paws on my gown. There was a viciousness about the animal that frightened me. Suddenly the door opened and a man appeared. He shouted to the dog, who to my intense relief ran off. I straightened my gown and cloak as the man stared hard at me.

18

This must be Seth Paslew, I thought. He was powerfully built, as befits an iron worker, hair black as jet and tied back with a ribbon. His features were strong and masculine, and in his voice there was the note of authority. There was no doubting who was master here.

"What do you want?" His expression was stern; no smile of welcome here.

"I'm Leah's sister, Damaris. I've come to see her. I wrote to say I was coming."

His expression deepened into a scowl.

"So the letter was from you. She's not here! She left last autumn!"

CHAPTER 2

"Last autumn?" I repeated incredulously.

"Yes. It would be November."

"Where did she go?"

It was his turn now to look surprised.

"She went back home, of course."

"Leah did not come home. We haven't seen her since"—I found it painful to speak of it—"Since she eloped. But did you not think to write to her?"

"What was the point? My letters would be unwelcome." He spoke in a flat, dispirited voice.

I felt drained and empty.

An old man appeared at the door. He wore an old blue coat fastened with wooden buttons, and cloth gaiters around his legs. At his neck was a soiled neckcloth. He was tall, like Seth Paslew, but his clothes hung on his bony frame. He wore his gray hair loose and untidy. I thought he looked ill.

"Whose this?" he demanded ungraciously.

"Leah's sister, father," answered Seth Paslew. "She's come to see her."

"She's gone," he said, waving his hand toward me, and

from the expression on his face I felt he wished me to go too. Then he turned, muttering to himself as he walked slowly back into the house.

"What shall I do?" I asked, feeling helpless.

"We don't encourage strangers at Wath Riding," he said coldly. "You'll find lodgings in the village."

It was a long way to the village. Could he really be so cruel as to send me down that lonely road in the dusk? I picked up my baggage with a heavy heart, and as I turned to go I saw a female face at a window. She knocked on the glass, motioning me to wait, and in a moment appeared at the door. She was short and stout with a homely face. Wisps of gray hair strayed from beneath her white cap, and over her skirt she had tied a piece of sacking to keep it clean. She regarded Seth Paslew sternly.

"Master Seth, ye're not going to send the lass away. All them miles over moor, and it's almost dark. Ye can at least offer her a bite of supper and a bed for the night."

"Bella, you're an interfering old harridan, and I'll be rid of you one of these days. Give Mistress Nunroyd a bed for the night, if that's what you want, but I want her gone by sunrise."

Then, without another word, he walked away.

Seething with indignation at his uncivilized behavior, I hesitated. There was still time to go. Still time to trudge the moorland road in the gathering gloom. At least I would be welcomed at the inn. But I weakened. I was tired, and I followed Bella into the house. It was a decision that altered the whole course of my life.

Bella led me down a long stone-flagged passage. The light was dim in here, and the place smelled none too clean. At the end of the passage there were two stone steps leading up to a door. She opened it and revealed the stairs—wide, shallow steps of polished wood. We climbed them, with Bella leading the way, puffing and panting, and at the top they curved around into a small semicircle. Over the staircase, the last of the pale evening light filtered through a small window.

We were now in a long corridor, with numerous doors leading off, and at the end was the circular window I had noticed from outside the house. Bella opened the first door, and we entered.

It was a small but clean room. In one corner stood an old table. The mirror that graced its surface was beautiful, with a silver frame of intricate design. I felt sure that at one time such a mirror had adorned a table far superior to the present one.

To the right of the table was a small window that faced north onto the moor. On the other side of the room was a cupboard reaching from floor to ceiling, taking up the entire wall. Bella opened it, and to my surprise it concealed a bed covered with a patchwork quilt. In the wall was a small window with a wide stone sill. I had heard of cupboard beds in old farmhouses but I had never seen one before.

"You'll be alright in the cupboard bed," said Bella, noticing my surprise. Then her eyes ran over my expensive gown.

"There's nothing grand here, mistress. You'll have to take us as you find us."

"I'm sure I'll sleep very well here, and thank you for your kindly intervention with your master. I'll be gone in the morning. I don't want to be any trouble to you."

"You're no trouble," she replied cheerfully. There was a softness in her face I liked.

"I'll bring ye up some water. Ye'll be wanting to have a

wash afore supper."

She left the room and I took off my wet cloak and hung it on a peg behind the door. As I did so, I noticed a curtain-covered alcove. The curtain was not fully drawn, and behind it I could see a familiar cream-lace gown. It was the gown in which Leah had eloped. I touched it gently with my fingers. There seemed something so sad and forlorn about it. There were other traces of Leah about the room. A pair of shoes beneath the bed; a green ribbon in the table drawer; a crumpled pocket handkerchief beneath the pillow.

How strange she had not slept with her husband!

Bella returned with the water. I said nothing to her, for after all, the private affairs of my sister and her husband, were not my concern.

After a quick wash, I combed my hair, straightened my gown, and went downstairs, not without a certain amount of trepidation, for Seth Paslew's intimidating manner had made me somewhat ill-at-ease.

The ground-floor passage now had a lighted lantern hanging from the ceiling, casting its pale beam on the bare white-washed walls. But where was supper being served? There was complete silence in the house, almost as if I were its only inmate.

I opened a door and peered in. The room appeared empty, and a cobweb touched my face. I hastily brushed it away and closed the door. I tried another door, but this was locked. Somehow I felt I was intruding on family secrets.

Suddenly I caught sight of Bella bearing a tray of food at the end of the passage. She had removed the sacking from around her waist and had changed her cap. With a sense of relief I quickly followed her.

We entered a small room, obviously the dining parlor, for the two men were seated at an oak table in the center of the room. The walls were paneled in black oak, and there were two small windows looking out onto the front courtyard. The floor was bare.

No one looked up as we entered, and Bella motioned me to a place she had set opposite the old man. Seth Paslew sat at the head of the table, and on my right a fourth place had been set. Who it was for?

Bella set steaming bowls of soup before us. It had a most appetizing smell, and I suddenly realized I was very hungry. We ate in silence. It was an unpleasant meal for I could feel the hostile atmosphere. I was the unwanted guest. I did not like the dark, morose expression on Seth Paslew's face, and when I looked across the table at the old man, I caught a look of despair.

A solitary candle burned in the center of the table, highlighting our faces and casting dark shadows in the corners of the room. Seth Paslew poured wine into the pewter goblets. He had changed into a finely embroidered waistcoat of bottle-green silk, decorated with silver buttons, which contrasted oddly with the old man's threadbare clothes. He pushed a goblet of wine toward me. The only wine drunk on this moor would be contraband, I thought. My pious, law-abiding father would not have it in the house. I took a sip. At least the wine was excellent.

Seth Paslew drank two goblets, and I watched his mood change. The tension in his face relaxed.

"Get Jack Reddihough to help you with the shearing, father," he was saying. "I'll help you if I can, but I may not be able to spare the time."

I pricked up my ears. "I may not be able to spare the

time!" What could he do on this lonely moor but attend to the sheep?

We certainly dined well. There was grouse cooked in wine, followed by boiled mutton and cabbage. Then Bella brought in a dish of cheese cakes. They were delicious.

"These cakes are the best I have ever tasted," I complimented her. "What are they called?"

"Richmond maids of honor," she replied proudly.

"How did they get such a name?"

"Oh, its a tale my grandmother used to tell," she said. "When King Henry married the great whore, the royal party went hunting at Richmond, here in Yorkshire. Anne Boleyn and her maids of honor were served these cakes, and they asked the king to try one. 'Ee,' he said, 'they're champion. What are they called?' Well, no one knew, so he christened them 'Richmond maids of honor.'"

"A delightful story!" I said. At least Bella spoke to me.

When we finished eating we went into the parlor across the passage. The two men seated themselves before a sluggishly burning peat fire, and I sat in a rocking chair. Neither man spoke to me, and from time to time the old man cast suspicious glances in my direction. I had never felt so unwanted.

Where was Leah? Where could she have gone?

The old man smoked his pipe and Seth Paslew helped himself to a large measure of brandy while they discussed the possibilities of good weather on the morrow. I looked around the room. It was large and oak paneled. The floor was bare stone and required sweeping, and candle grease had been spilled everywhere.

Against one wall was an oak dresser displaying a fine set of blue and white Delft plates. There was a chest against another wall—a fine piece of craftsmanship, heavily carved with a design of leaves. To my surprise there were books scattered haphazardly about the room. I bent down and read one of the titles. It was *The Complete Works of William Shakespeare*. How strange! Usually the only book one saw in these farmhouses was the family Bible. There was no sign of Seth Paslew's family Bible.

As I rocked myself gently to and fro, I began to feel that there was something odd about this farm and its occupants. In the first place, Seth Paslew was too well dressed for a man in his position. Secondly, the food we had just eaten was the food one could expect at a far richer man's table. In the cottages I had passed on the road that evening, the meal would be a bit of fried bacon. And thirdly, Seth Paslew appeared unconcerned about his wife's disappearance.

Could Seth Paslew have made her so unhappy she had run away? If that was the case, my presence would be a distinct embarrassment to him.

What could have happened to her? Everyone Leah knew lived in Calverley, and I knew she was not there. What could I tell them at home? She was missing? I looked at Seth Paslew, who was discussing sheep with his father. Just a normal conversation about the latest market prices, as any son would have with his father, yet I felt it was for my benefit.

After a while, the old man said he was tired and shuffled unsteadily from the room. Now I was alone with Seth Paslew, and I did not like it, but I had to speak to him about Leah.

"Mr. Paslew, you do not appear at all worried about my sister's disappearance."

"Up to your arrival a few hours ago, I thought she was

26

at Calverley. What do you want me to do? Call out the dragoons?''

There was something disturbing about him, and he was drinking far too much brandy. I wondered how drunk he was. I was a fool to have stayed. His shirt sleeves were rolled up, and the hairs on his arms were thick and black.

"I've got enough worries without thinking about Leah," he said staring into the fire. "My God, I feel depressed tonight. I must have been born under an unlucky star."

His gaze turned to the bare floor, and then to the dresser.

"Those Delft plates belong to my grandmother. They're the only things worth having in this house. The rest—it went long ago."

His voice was filled with self pity as he continued: "We once owned a third of Wathdale. Does that surprise you? Been in the family since Edward III's time. A wounded boar charged the king's horse, and my ancestor, one Robert de Paslew slayed the boar and saved the king's life. His reward was Wath Riding.

"And what have we now . . . we have nothing, thanks to my improvident ancestors and their stupidity. Bad blood, some call it. Bit by bit the land was sold off to pay their debts. Now the Paslews pay rent to the landlord."

Suddenly he rose to his feet and glared at me with such a wild look in his eyes I could feel myself shrinking back in the chair.

"I want that land back," he shouted. "I'm hungry for it. And I want all the things it will give me—power and freedom and beauty."

He drained the goblet of brandy.

"One day I shall get it all back, down to the last acre."

27

Then he fell lengthways onto the settle, and his eyes closed.

Rising as quietly as I could, I tiptoed across the room. Now was my chance to escape.

"Mistress Nunroyd."

He startled me so, I nearly jumped.

"I have told you my ambition, and what is yours?"

He was lying on the settle in such a way that I could not see him.

"It—it's not as grand as yours," I stammered nervously.

Then I stopped. My thoughts were too private to tell a stranger.

"Go on," he commanded. "I'm waiting."

"I—I just want to make people happy."

I waited for him to pour scorn on me, but he did not.

"It's a pity your fine father didn't have those sentiments. Making his daughter penniless so I wouldn't lay a finger on his precious brass. Not good enough for him, eh. Well, I'll show him."

"You must excuse my father, but he thought he was doing the best for Leah. He should never have behaved as he did. You were good enough. I believe all men are equal."

I was amazed at myself. I had never told a living person my private thoughts before.

"That's revolutionary talk. You're a rebel."

I closed the door behind me and went upstairs. I could still hear him laughing. Whatever possessed me to speak to him as I did? I could not understand myself.

I undressed slowly, thinking about him. He was certainly a man of surprises, but his ambitions astounded me. How could he hope to buy back the Paslew land? The magnitude of his ambition utterly outstripped his earning power, and yet he seemed so sure he would do it.

I opened the cupboard and crept into bed. Seth Paslew had a personal magnetism that both excited and repelled. Had my sister felt that too? And who had the fourth place been set for at supper? Whoever it was, they had not come.

It was impossible to sleep. After a while I sat up and leaned my elbows on the window sill. My room was at the rear of the house and looked directly onto the barn and stable.

The moonlight was so bright I could see that the top of the barn entrance was in need of repair. The stones had tumbled down and lay in a pile on the ground. The stable door was open and I thought I could hear the whinnying of a horse inside. Above the stable door, the wooden shutter for the loft opening hung on one hinge, and as the evening breeze stirred the shutter banged rhythmically againt the wall.

Seth Paslew and his father could not even keep their rented farm in good repair. Perhaps all that talk of buying back the farm was just "brandy talk," as my father would say.

The barn and stable blocked my view of the lake. It probably looked beautiful on such a night as this, I thought. Suddenly I heard a step below my window, and to my surprise Seth Paslew walked across the yard, disappearing around the corner of the barn. He was walking quickly as if in a great hurry.

Instantly my curiosity was aroused. Where could he be going at this time of night, and in such a hurry?

Slipping into my shoes, I flung my cloak quickly around my shoulders. All my instincts told me I could be doing something foolish, perhaps dangerous, but I chose to ignore them.

Opening the door slowly, I crept down the stairs. Moonlight filtered through the window, casting a silver light on the old polished steps. As I opened the stairs door it gave a sickening creak which made my heart miss a beat. I did not wish to disturb Bella or the old man. What explanation could I give?

At last, out of the house, I tiptoed across the yard and around the barn. Overhead, clouds moved silently across the sky. Beyond the barn was a low stone wall with a stile. As I climbed it I heard the sudden cry of an animal in pain.

There was no sign of Seth Paslew in that vast moon-drenched landscape. I followed the path through the heather, the ground rising, and when I reached the top of the slope, the lake lay before me. For a brief moment I forgot the reason for my nocturnal walk as I gazed at the shimmering silver water in the moonlight. There were a few pine trees growing near the shore, their slender silhouettes black against the silver water. It was the loveliest sight I had ever seen.

Suddenly I caught sight of him, walking along the path that skirted the lake. He was walking in the direction of a small stone cottage on the opposite shore, probably an unused shepherd's hut. Beyond the cottage was the dark cloud of a small wood in a hollow.

After what seemed an interminable length of time, he reached the cottage, and to my amazement, from out of the shadows, a dark figure on horseback appeared, dismounted, and followed Seth Paslew into the cottage.

A cold wind sprang up from the lake, rippling its surface, and I found myself shivering.

CHAPTER 3

Suddenly I felt afraid. The courage that had brought me to this spot deserted me. If Seth Paslew and the stranger came out of the cottage now and saw me standing on the high ground above the lake, what might they do?

I started to run. I should never have followed him, I told myself as I stumbled over the stony path. My sense of curiosity was too strong, and one day it would get me into trouble.

I reached the ridge above Wath Riding. With horror, I saw the dark silhouette of a man moving toward me. He was climbing slowly with a curious swinging movement. There were some bushes nearby, and flinging myself on the grass behind them I lay with panting heart while he approached. He drew level with me and passed, following the path down to the lake, and as I peeked at his retreating figure I realized he had the characteristic gait of a man with a wooden leg.

I started running down the slope. There must have been a large stone in the path for suddenly I tripped and fell. I rose shakily to my feet, and to my intense

annoyance, my ankle hurt.

I continued down the path, hobbling now, for my ankle was quite painful and my progress slow. Gradually I became aware of the sound of running water. Just what I needed to sooth my aching ankle. I paused and scanned the moorland to see where the beck could be. Then suddenly I saw it—about twenty yards away, and hobbling across as best I could, I sat down upon its bank.

The beck was running down the hillside in a series of little waterfalls, the moonlight turning the water to molten silver. Taking off my shoe and stocking, I held my painful ankle in the icy cold water. Then, taking the neckerchief from around my neck, I dipped it in the water, rung it out, and tied it around my ankle.

Suddenly I heard the sound of voices. The dark figures of Seth Paslew and the man with the wooden leg were moving down the slope. I lay flat in the heather, motionless, my heart thumping so against my ribs I thought I would faint. I held my breath as I heard their footsteps drawing nearer, then gradually they receded into the distance, growing fainter and fainter, until I could no longer hear them.

I lay there for a long time, too frightened to move. Then a cloud passed over the moon making the moor a dark and secret thing. I shivered; if I had minded my own business I could have been lying in that cozy bed in Wath Riding instead of out here on the cold and lonely moor. What right had I to pry into this man's private affairs anyway? I had every right, I reasoned to myself; I had the right to know what happened to my sister.

Feeling it was now safe to continue, I slowly rose to my feet. My ankle felt more comfortable, but it was still painful, and I continued on my way.

I climbed the stile slowly, walked past the barn, and entered the farmyard. The house was in darkness, as I expected, and, walking as noiselessly as I could across the cobblestones, I tried the kitchen door.

It was locked!

Seth Paslew must have drawn the bolt when he came in. I would have to spend the rest of the night in either the stable loft or the barn.

Fearing the presence of a stranger would upset the horse, I chose the barn. The great double doors were open, and I peered into the gloomy interior. There was a small stack of peat, a pile of hay, and a farm cart. Sinking wearily onto the hay, I fell asleep immediately, and in my dreams I saw Leah. She was alone and frightened and calling for me.

I awoke next morning to a soft May day. Bright sunshine flooded the barn entrance, and a swallow glided in through the open entrance. I felt stiff and tired and my head ached as I watched the bird fly up to its nest in the raftered roof.

Seth Paslew had said I must be gone by sunrise. It was long past that now. But I did not want to return home. I dreaded meeting my father and the questions he would ask. And how could I go back to Calverley and pick up the threads of my old life, feeling that something terrible had happened to Leah?

I stood up and put my weight on my ankle. It was much better, but the pain was still there. Then I looked down at my gown and cloak. They were so badly creased and stained I looked like a scarecrow.

I was still thinking about Leah as I walked out of the barn, scattering the hens as I went. I decided to speak to

Bella. She might know something.

Suddenly a horse whinnied in the stable. Opening the stable door, I went in. There were two stalls. One was empty, and the other contained a fine-looking chestnut mare with a white mark on its forehead.

As I entered she moved forward and nuzzled me, glad of company. She seemed to be a thoroughbred. I was surprised. I was expecting to find an old cart horse or a half-starved pony. There was a bucket hanging on the wall, and, taking it down, I walked across to the well in the yard. As I lowered the bucket into the water, I noticed that the apple tree was pink with blossom, and a few yards beyond the tree bees buzzed about the beehive wall.

A voice startled me, and I turned to find the old man standing there. There was gray stubble on his chin and that look of defeat was still in his eyes. I think I knew before the old man spoke that I would not be on the stagecoach from Settle that day.

He regarded my disheveled appearance curiously for a moment as I drew up the water.

"That for Roxanna?" he asked.

I nodded.

"Here, I'll take it."

As he took the bucket from me he remarked with suspicion: "You're up early. Didn't hear you come down."

I followed him silently into the stable. How could I tell him I had been spying on his son and been locked out!

"Bella's ill." He sounded depressed.

"What's the matter with her?" I asked, taking the empty bucket from him.

He shook his head.

"She's bad."

"I'll go to her," I said. "Where is her room?"

"Up the kitchen stairs," he said, nodding toward the back door.

The kitchen was large and stone flagged, with whitewashed walls and a window that looked onto the backyard. There was a square wooden table in the center of the room, and against one wall stood a wooden chest— the lid open showing it was half full of oatmeal. Overhead hung hams and bacon joints smoked to a dark brown, and the fire in the open hearth was nearly out.

I climbed the narrow staircase that led up from the kitchen, and walked into a room under the rafters, its walls crudely and unevenly plastered.

The only furniture in the room was Bella's truckle bed covered with a faded pink knitted cover, and by the bedside a small cupboard containing, no doubt, her worldly possessions. She lay on the pillow wearing an old nightgown so patched and darned it was beyond any further repair. Her long gray hair was unpinned and spread out over the pillow. There was no color in her face, and her hands, ugly and strong, that had known a lifetime's drudgery, lay limply on the bedcover.

"Bella!" I exclaimed, full of concern, walking toward the bed. "Whatever is the matter?"

"It's me belly, Mistress Damaris," she said. "Pain's so bad that sometimes . . ."

Suddenly she clutched herself as a spasm of pain took possession of her. When it had passed, she looked wearily up at me, and whispered: "It's that devil downstairs what done this. He's poisoned me food."

"You mean the old man?" I asked, astounded.

She lowered her voice until it was barely audible.

"I know too much."

37

I thought that Bella was hysterical as a result of the suffering she was enduring.

"You need a physician, Bella."

"I don't want no physician. Get Jinny. She'll know what to do."

"Where do I find her?"

"A couple of miles up yonder."

She meant to the north, I thought, for I did not remember passing a cottage on the moor when I came with the carrier.

"I'll go immediately."

"I'm that glad you're here, Mistress Damaris. You're as kind as Mistress Leah."

Leah! I could not speak to Bella about her now. It would have to wait.

I retraced my steps down the long stone staircase to the kitchen below. The old man was there, kneeling at the hearth, working the bellows. Bella had to be mistaken. He looked like just a weary old man.

"Bella wants me to go to Jinny's," I said.

He stopped working the bellows and looked up at me.

"You mean Jinny Thirkettle, the wise woman. She'll do her best for Bella."

I did not care to limp a few miles on a sore ankle, so I asked the old man if I could go on Roxanna. Begrudgingly, he gave his permission.

Walking across to the stable, I noticed that there was no sign of Seth Paslew. Perhaps he was a late riser. A strange man, I thought as I saddled up Roxanna, then leading her out into the sunshine. She stood patiently while I mounted her.

In a few minutes we were on the moorland road. Roxanna was gentle and well mannered. Quite different

38

from her master, I thought. It was a beautiful day, warm and sunny, with just a light wind whispering across the moor. Two hares appeared from nowhere and ran a mad, joyous race across the heather. A pheasant, that lovely long-tailed bird, rose from a clump of bracken and flew low over the moor, disappearing into a hollow. Yesterday the loneliness of Wath Moor had chilled me; today I found it exhilarating for it was a bright, living thing.

The road dipped, and I saw Jinny Thirkettle's cottage. It was similar to the one I had seen the night before by the lake—a small, one-story stone structure set back from the road. A garden had been valiantly reclaimed from the moor; here she grew her vegetables, flowers, and herbs.

I stopped at the gate and dismounted. Jinny appeared in the open doorway. She was a small, frail-looking old woman, but her features were sharp, her dark eyes bright and quick. When she opened her mouth, there wasn't a tooth in her head. Her gray hair hung long and straight to her shoulders. She was dressed in a faded lavender-striped gown, frayed and torn at the hem. And she was knitting, with a tossing motion peculiar to this part of the world. A knitting sheath shaped like a goose wing was fitted to the leather belt around her waist, and on this sheath was a hook on which the knitting was suspended to prevent it from trailing on the ground.

"Are you Jinny Thirkettle?" I asked nervously.

There had been a wise woman like Jinny at Calverley before I was born. My mother told me she had been accused of witchcraft and hanged by the townspeople.

"I'm Jinny Thirkettle," she said.

"Bella at Wath Riding sent me. She's ill, and she said you'd know what to do."

She considered this a moment before replying.

"You'd best come into the house."

I tied Roxanna's reins to the gate, and followed Jinny into the one-room cottage. The light was dim, there being only one small window, and when I became accustomed to the gloom a curious sight met my eyes. Hanging from the ceiling were hundreds of bunches of herbs, like a tiny forest, their collective smell strange, sweet and pungent. Hanging on a nail behind the door was a necklace of stones, which I knew was to protect her from evil. Sitting before the fire was a fine-looking black cat.

"Sit yerself down on buffet," Jinny said kindly, motioning me to a three-legged stool by the fire. "I'll make a pot of tea while you tell me about it."

"You're very kind, Jinny," I said, sitting. How silly of me to have been afraid of her.

I watched her unlock the tea caddy on the mantel. Obviously there was plenty of contraband tea as well as wine and brandy on this moor. I wondered how the deliveries were made.

"She has a bad pain in her stomach," I said. I did not repeat Bella's wild accusations. "She was well yesterday evening, so the pain must have started during the night. As far as I know, no one else in the house is ill."

She handed me a cup of tea. It was strong and sweet, and as I sipped the scalding liquid I could feel it putting new life into me. She went to a small cupboard across the room, took out a small linen bag and handed it to me. I opened it curiously. The contents looked like a fine green powder.

"It's only an herb," she said, smiling. "Brew it like tea, and give it to her three times a day. Three days from now she'll be right as rain."

"Thank you, Jinny," I said, and I handed her a few

40

coins for her trouble.

"What you doing at Wath Riding?" she regarded me curiously.

"I'm Leah's sister. I came to see her, but she's gone!" A strange, incomprehensible look clouded her eyes.

"I know, and if you know what's good for you, you'll go too. Them Paslews got bad blood. 'Tis no place for a young lass on her own. Things happen on this moor 'tis best not talked about."

Then the old woman moved toward the door to denote the interview was over. As I followed her I noticed a leather bag on her window sill. It was bright red in color, with green draw strings.

"Poisonous herbs," she said, noticing my interest. "I put them in a red bag, so there's no mistaking them."

She opened it, and tipped some of the contents into her hand.

"Foxglove seeds," she said. "Cures dropsy, but if you takes too much, it kills."

When we reached the gate, I turned back to admire a particular flower Jinny was discussing, when I noticed a stone carving of a man's head on the wall of the cottage just below the eaves.

"What is that?" I asked.

"I belongs to the old religion," she replied, as if that explained everything.

"The old religion?"

She nodded solemnly.

"The one before Christianity. We worshipped the earth."

I looked at her, startled and intrigued.

"It's nothing to do with witchcraft or sorcery," she continued. "But the people here don't understand that.

41

That's why they hanged my mother from the tree. They said she was a witch."

"I am sorry, Jinny," I said.

"Be sorry for them that done it."

Waving farewell to Jinny, I trotted off down the lonely moorland road. How could one meet an English woman in the eighteenth century who did not believe in Christianity? But, although I was a Christian, in some strange way I could understand her worshipping the earth.

As I reached Wath Riding I wondered what happened on this moor that Jinny could not talk about. I put Roxanna into the stable, and walked into the kitchen. There was no one about.

I boiled the water as Jinny had instructed, and made the herbal tea, then took a cup of it up to Bella.

She was pleased to see me. I put the cup into her hand and she sipped the tea slowly.

"Jinny allus gets you right when you're ill," she said when she had finished drinking. Then she lay back on the pillow and smiled weakly at me.

"Had any more pain?" I asked her.

She nodded.

"You'll not be leaving just yet, will ye, mistress?"

Her eyes beseeched me to stay.

"I'll stay, Bella," I assured her.

She closed her eyes. Poor Bella, she looked so weary. I tiptoed out and made my way to my room. Passing a mirror I saw that I looked like a gypsy with my dirty clothes and uncombed hair. I quickly changed into a simple linen gown. I thought it suitable for a farm, and it was my favorite color. The color of a summer sky. Then I combed my long, tangled hair.

Feeling much better, I went downstairs. As I opened the stairs door, I heard Seth Paslew speaking to his father.

"You say Bella's ill," he was saying. "What's the matter with her—got the pox?"

The voices were coming from the front parlor, and as I passed the entrance the men turned and stared at me.

"You still here?" Seth Paslew's voice was curt.

I took a deep breath.

"I have promised Bella I will stay until she is better."

He pursed his lips.

"Still the rebel?"

He is at liberty to throw me out if he wishes, I thought.

"She needs attention," I continued. "I cannot walk out and leave her."

"When will she be better?"

"Jinny says in three days."

"Then see you leave this house as soon as she is better. Why are you limping?"

I could feel my heart beating like a sledgehammer. Did he know I had followed him last night?

"I slipped on the kitchen stairs this morning."

I wasn't good at lying. His face was immobile. I could not tell what he was thinking.

"I want this place clean. I've got an important meeting here tonight."

The old man followed him out of the room like a lap dog.

Seth Paslew was impossible, I fumed to myself when the door was closed. How dare he treat me as if I were a common servant girl. And how violently his moods could change. The intimate atmosphere of last night had gone.

I found a broom and started sweeping the dirty floor of

the front parlor, more from a desire to help Bella than Seth Paslew. He made me more angry than any man I had ever met. I picked up the books that were scattered about the room and stacked them neatly on top of the chest. His tastes were certainly unusual for a man of his background. There was Homer's *Iliad*, Laurence Sterne's *Tristram Shandy*, and Milton's *Paradise Lost*.

By lunchtime the room was swept and dusted, and the candle grease scraped from floor and furniture. I was exhausted. I had never worked so hard in my life, but as I surveyed the room, I was pleased with my efforts.

I made another herbal brew for Bella and took it up to her room, helping her to hold the cup, and when she had drunk all she wanted, she lay back on the pillows and slept. If this herbal tea did not work the miracle Jinny had promised, I would have to get the physician from Settle.

I was putting some peat on the kitchen fire when the door opened and Seth Paslew entered. I was surprised to see he had changed and was wearing a traveling coat of deep blue and a black tricorne upon his head. He had secured a belt around his waist and into this had slung a pistol.

"I've an urgent business trip to make," he announced. "I won't be back until late tonight."

He picked up his saddlebag—I noticed it was very bulky—and moved toward the door.

"And while you're here, ignore the ravings of Bella. She's just an old fool, and if you repeat one word of her blatherings to anyone, you'll wish you'd never been born."

Then he closed the door. I did not move, for his words had rooted me to the spot. Was this the same man who last night had confided in me his intimate thoughts? How could one trust such a man?

From the side window I watched him ride along the moorland road toward the village. When he was lost from view, I felt a sudden sense of release, as if I had been freed from some bondage. I took the dishes that were stacked on the table and put them in a store cupboard. I was not going to let a man like Seth Paslew scare me. I had more courage than that.

At the kitchen door I shooed the hens off the step. I would have to find out where they laid their eggs. On the moor to the south I could see the man and the collie in the far distance. The dog was a black and white flash as she darted to and fro rounding up the flock.

Now was my chance. Bella was sleeping comfortably. It would take the old man a long time to round up the scattered flock, and Seth Paslew was gone until late that night. As I set off up the moorland path that would lead me to the lake my spirits rose. The heather would soon be in bloom, staining the moor purple with its flower. I felt I had made the right decision to visit the lake cottage, for in my mind it was linked with Leah's disappearance. Without realizing it, I was being drawn deeper into the web.

CHAPTER 4

I reached the top of the ridge and paused. The lake lay before me, blue and calm, and I started walking down the sloping path that would lead me to the water's edge. The little cottage came into view on the far shore, blinking innocently in the midday sun, and behind it, the wood, rich, green, and cool, filled the hollow.

Beyond the lake the moor stretched in every direction, and at the horizon, the fells rose misty and blue. As the clouds scurried across the sky, the colors of the moor constantly changed.

Soon I had drawn level with the cottage where, the night before, I had seen Seth Paslew and the horseman. It was a poor, humble place, with a stone, slate roof sagging gently in the middle, and patches of green moss.

I tried the door, but to my disappointment it was locked. I then tried to look in through the little window, but the dust was so thick upon the pane that I had to take out my pocket handkerchief and rub it clean.

To my surprise I looked into a blacksmith's workshop. There was a workbench immediately beneath the window, but it was bare of any tools. Against one wall was

46

a wooden chest, and in the opposite wall an open hearth. By the side of the hearth was an anvil, and hanging on hooks on the wall were a range of horses' shoes, chains, and other paraphernalia. Seth Paslew was the local blacksmith! Not surprising, since he was a skilled iron worker.

My disappointment was intense. I don't know what I expected to find, but certainly not a blacksmith's shop. There was obviously no connection here with Leah.

Turning sadly away, I wandered into the wood behind the cottage. The trees were so close together, the light that filtered through the leaves was pale green. It was like being under water, and the cow parsley that grew between the trees looked like fragments of lace. Leah called it "old man's tobacco," but I preferred its proper name. I picked a bunch to put in Bella's room, then wandered disconsolately back to the cottage.

Suddenly I heard the sound of approaching horse's hooves, and looking across the lake I saw a horseman riding along the south shore. For a brief, frightening moment I thought it was Seth Paslew. The rider kept to the path that encircled the lake, and as he drew nearer I could not help feeling apprehensive, for in that vast landscape there was no other living soul in sight.

As he approached I recognized with surprise the man who had sat opposite me in the stagecoach yesterday. He was wearing the same brown coat, but he was now hatless.

He pulled up his horse a few yards from me; there was still that strange look of sorrow in his eyes. He looked at me, puzzled for a moment, before recognition dawned.

"You're the young lady from the stagecoach!"

He dismounted and walked toward me.

"I'm Christian Malloughby. My great uncle owns this land."

His face creased into a pleasant grin.

I frowned. Was he going to tell me I was trespassing?

He unstrapped his saddlebag and sat down upon the grassy bank by the shore.

"Do you live here?" he asked casually.

"No. I'm a visitor at Wath Riding."

I noticed his lips tighten, but he said nothing, looking across the lake watching the sun glittering gold on the water.

I started to move away; I had lingered long enough.

"I must be getting back to Wath Riding," I said hurriedly. I was not accustomed to speaking to strange men. "If you will excuse me."

"Don't go!" His voice was urgent and beseeching. "Would you like to share my picnic lunch? I hate eating alone."

What a strange request!

From his saddlebag he brought out a white linen cloth, unfolded it and revealed a cold chicken, salad, and a bottle of wine. It certainly looked very tempting, for all I had consumed that day was a cup of tea at Jinny Thirkettle's. I think I accepted because I felt a strong need to talk to someone, and I liked his face. It was kind and sympathetic.

The sun was warm by the lakeside, and soon Christian Malloughby's easy-going manner relaxed me.

"You look like a well-brought-up young English woman," he commented, handing me a leg of chicken. "Consequently, you must consider me extremely unconventional inviting a stranger to lunch with me."

"I do," I smiled, taking a bite.

"Where I come from we are less formal about such matters."

"Where do you come from?" I inquired. I could not confess I had eavesdropped on his conversation in the coach.

"Virginia."

"Virginia! You have traveled a very great distance, Mr. Malloughby. What brings you to Yorkshire, may I ask?"

"It's a long story and a sad one. Do you want to hear it?"

"I do," I said.

"Well, my grandfather, Josiah Malloughby, was born at Winterburn Hall. He was the second son, so he didn't inherit. The custom was to enter the church, or the army, or become a lawyer. Well, grandfather Josiah didn't want to do any of those things. He was an adventurous young man, and amazed the family by saying he wanted to go to America and become a tobacco planter. They thought he was mad, but he persisted, and in the end he got his way. So he emigrated to America, got himself a nice plantation on the James River, and married a Virginian girl. My father was born. Father grew up and married, and my brother Widd and I were born. Unfortunately, father died when we were children.

"Widd was different from me. He was the restless, adventurous type, like grandfather. The old man was always talking to him about the old country, and the house in Yorkshire where he had lived as a boy. I can see them now, on the porch in the evening. Grandfather going over the old stories. Of course, Widd had heard them all before, and sometimes he'd say 'Grandfather, I shall go there one day.' So last year, when grandfather died, I wasn't surprised when Widd announced he was going to England. 'When I've done a bit of traveling around,' he said, 'I'll come back, and settle down to tobacco planting for the rest of my life.' So off he went.

"His letters in the beginning were full of enthusiasm about the wonderful places he saw in England. Then he came up to Yorkshire and met Uncle Matthew, who was grandfather's brother. They seemed to get along fine. In fact, I wondered if he was going to come back; he seemed so happy here. Then, in his last letter, he said he had come across some criminal activity and wanted to stamp it out. It was causing distress among the people, and could become a danger to the country. I only wish he had told me what it was."

Christian Malloughby stopped, gazing pensively across the water as if his thoughts were too painful to continue.

"What happened to your brother, Mr. Malloughby?" I asked gently.

"His body was found at the foot of Wath Cliff, not far from here."

So it was Christian Malloughby's brother that the carrier had referred to!

"There was an inquiry, and the verdict was suicide," he continued. "Widd would never commit suicide. He enjoyed living too much. I knew my brother better than anyone. We were very close. Suicide—that is something Widd would never do. I believe he was murdered. That's why I've come here. I want Widd's murderer brought to justice."

"Why should anyone want to murder him?"

"Perhaps he knew too much, so someone pushed him over Wath Cliff."

We sat there in silence for a while. I was appalled at what Christian Malloughby had just told me. He struck

51

me as being a calm, logical sort of person, not one who jumps to wild conclusions, and I had no reason to doubt his views.

"People are too frightened to talk. The butler Beckwith at Winterburn Hall knows something—I'm sure of it."

He picked up a pebble and skimmed it across the surface of the water.

"Are you staying long at Wath Riding?" he asked casually.

"I don't know," I replied. "You see, I came to visit my sister, and when I arrived Seth Paslew told me she had left in November—gone home, he said, but she had not returned home."

I paused, frowning at the memory of it.

"How strange! What do you think has happened to her?"

"I don't know."

"She could have gone to visit friends?"

"I don't think so. The only people Leah knew live in Calverley."

"I'm sure you'll find there'll be some reasonable explanation to the whole matter. What's in the cottage?"

"Oh nothing—Seth Paslew uses it for blacksmith work."

"Would you like some more chicken or wine?"

"No, thank you. I've had sufficient, and it was delicious."

"I nearly forgot about the fishing," he exclaimed suddenly, standing up. "Like to come? My uncle tells me this tarn is full of trout."

I hesitated.

"Come on," he urged. "Surely the thought of grilled

trout is enough to make your mouth water!"

I agreed. So many unusual things had happened in the past twenty-four hours that I was becoming accustomed to surprises, but above all, I liked his air of quiet confidence, and his straightforward manner. We started walking along the shore.

"There must be a boat and tackle somewhere," he said.

Suddenly I saw it moored at the water's edge, screened by hawthorn bushes.

"Two fishing lines are at the bottom. That's fortunate. No doubt the property of your brother-in-law; my uncle never comes near the tarn. Well, as I'll be borrowing his tackle, on this occasion I'll turn a blind eye to his poaching."

"Doesn't he rent the tarn?" I asked innocently.

"No. Uncle was showing me his accounts this morning. Seth Paslew just rents his farm, that cottage, and pays for grazing rights for a certain area of the moor."

I stepped gingerly into the rocking boat while Christian Malloughby took a small knife from his pocket and dug for worms at the water's edge. In a few minutes he held half a dozen wriggling, fat worms in his hand. I screwed up my nose.

"What a horrible sight," I laughed, as he stepped in and sat down. I must be quite mad, I thought. First I have lunch with a strange man, and then I go fishing with him. If my mother knew, she would be extremely alarmed.

Picking up an oar, Christian pushed the boat away from the shore, then, picking up the other, rowed smoothly toward the center of the lake.

"You haven't told me your name yet," he said,

grinning at me.

"Damaris," I replied. "Damaris Nunroyd."

He rowed very well, as if he had been doing it all his life. I trailed my hand in the cold water as we glided along. There wasn't a breath of wind, and the only sound was the oars rhythmically smacking the water. This young man had a soothing effect upon me, and I liked it. He rested his oars and smiled gently at me.

"Now we'll see if we have any luck with the fish."

He put the worm on my hook with an expertise born of practice.

"Do you fish often in Virginia?" I asked.

"As often as I can get away from the plantation," he replied.

I nervously started to lower my line into the water.

"I've never fished before," I confessed.

"Don't let it trail along the bottom, and keep quiet."

I watched him put the worm on his own hook, noticing how strong and capable his hands were. Wath Riding and its occupants seemed far away at that moment as I held the line. Suddenly I felt a tug.

"I've caught one," I cried exultantly, and all my attention was on the fish. I could see its silver body writhing and struggling in the water. I stood up and started hauling it in quickly.

"Slowly!"

Suddenly the trout twisted in the water and was gone.

"I've lost him," I groaned as I sat down. My disappointment was intense.

"I told you to haul in slowly."

I saw the pull on his line and watched him wind his line in slowly, and with great care, then expertly flip the fish into the bottom of the boat. It was a large rainbow trout.

It struggled for life for a few minutes, and then lay still.

"She's a beauty," he said with pride.

"She certainly is," I agreed.

"You must learn patience. You must learn to watch and wait, and try again. Well, I'm sorry to have to bring a delightful afternoon to a close, but we must go. My uncle is none too well and I promised I would not be long. We must go fishing again, and next time you must catch one, Damaris."

He picked up the oars and slowly rowed back to the shore. I had a feeling we were rowing back to reality. We secured the boat, leaving it hidden in the bushes as we had found it, and walked back to the lake cottage where Christian Malloughby had tethered his horse.

"Thank you, Mr. Malloughby. You've been very kind."

"Will you call me Christian?"

I nodded and smiled.

"You'll be home quicker if you ride pillion to the top of the ridge."

I agreed, for it was now late afternoon and I was starting to feel worried about Bella. Christian put the trout into his saddlebag and we mounted.

"It's most fortunate we met today," he said as we trotted along the shore. "For there is something I would like you to do." He looked very serious.

"I'll be pleased to help you."

"Watch out for anything suspicious at Wath Riding. Keep your ears and eyes open. Miss nothing. And if you do find out anything, send a message to me at Winterburn Hall, or better still, come yourself."

"Why do you think there should be anything suspicious at Wath Riding?"

"Because on the evening of Widd's death, he visited

Wath Riding. He told uncle he was going there, and I believe Seth Paslew was the last person to see him alive."

"I'll do my best," I assured him.

We had now reached the top of the ridge. Christian stopped his horse and I dismounted. Then, opening his saddlebag, he took out the trout and handed it to me.

"Here you are; a present from me. You can tell them that some poacher left it by the lake. You must go quickly. It is best if we are not seen together for we must not arouse suspicion. Goodbye, Damaris. Take care. And if you ever need my help, you know where to find me."

Turning his horse, he rode away.

I started walking down the moorland slope carrying the trout. Smoke was rising from the kitchen chimney of the farmhouse, and bleating noises came from the sheepfold at the back of the barn. The old man was nowhere to be seen.

If I kept to this path, it would lead me past the house, through the gate, and in a few minutes I would be on the moorland road. Within an hour I could be in the village. I could feel the few guineas I had brought with me jingling in the pocket of my gown. I could get lodgings for the night in the village, and the next morning catch the stagecoach at Settle.

As I climbed the stile I suddenly remembered I had left Bella's flowers on the lake shore. I walked past the barn and crossed the yard.

There was no running away. I had promised Christian I would help him, and as I approached the house I could hear Bella calling for me.

CHAPTER 5

I put the trout on the kitchen table and hurried up the narrow staircase to Bella's room.

"Oh, Mistress Damaris," she said as soon as I entered the room. "I'm glad to see you. My mouth's parched for want of a drink of water. I tried to get up, but my legs are like jelly."

I was full of contrition for my long absence.

"I'm sorry, Bella, I was away for such a long time. I'll get you a drink right away."

I went down to the kitchen. The large stone container that usually held drinking water was empty. So, taking a pail from a hook on the wall I went out to the well in the yard and drew up a fresh supply. Then, returning to Bella's room, I watched her drink the cool, fresh water.

When she finished she wiped her mouth with the back of her hand.

"That were good," she said with satisfaction.

"You're looking a little better, Bella," I commented, sitting on the bed.

"I am that. It's Jinny's herbs that done it. She's better than any of your fancy physicians."

I got up to go.

"Stay a while and talk to me. It gets lonely up here."

I sat down on the bed again. Could I talk to her about Leah? I decided to try.

"Tell me about Leah," I said in a quiet, coaxing voice. She was silent for a minute or two.

"She hurt me. She never said goodbye."

"You mean the day she left?"

Bella nodded.

"She were always with me in kitchen, helping out."

"Was there some trouble between Leah and Seth Paslew?"

She nodded.

"I never knew what it was. Wasn't my place to interfere."

"Did they quarrel?"

"He rarely spoke to her. But there were a quarrel night she went."

"I have to ask these questions because I'm concerned about my sister's disappearance. Did you hear what was said?"

"They were in front parlor with door closed. He were very angry, and their voices were sort of muffled. But I did hear Mistress Leah say, 'You must be insane.' I went to bed after that."

"And what did Seth Paslew say to that?"

"He just laughed."

"What did Leah mean when she told him he was insane?"

"I don't know. What he does is none of my business. I'm just his housekeeper." She looked agitated, and her fingers clutched nervously at the bed cover.

"Was Leah happy?"

"No."

There was a firmness about Bella's reply that disturbed me. Then there was a long silence. I felt she knew something but could not speak of it. Better to change the subject.

"How did Leah spend her time when she wasn't helping you?"

"She used to go for long walks on moor," Bella answered. "She worried me at times. I used to say to her, one day you'll get lost on them moors. Mist comes down suddenlike in wintertime. One minute you can see for miles and next you cannot see a hand before you. But she never took no notice of me. She talked a lot about you, and your mother, and your brother Jonathan. But she never mentioned your father."

Leah was not likely to. The wound was too deep.

"How long have you been working for the Paslews, Bella?"

"Oh, since I were a lass. I were twenty when I first come here, and Master Seth were only a lad. His mother were alive then. She were a nice lady, fair and just. If she saw I were tired, she'd say, 'Leave it Bella, leave it till morning.' She wouldn't work you until you were ready to drop—like them two." Bella looked toward the top of the stairs and scowled.

Then her expression changed and she gave a chuckle.

"I've given Master Seth many a walloping when he were little."

"Did you ever want to marry, Bella?"

A faraway look came into Bella's eyes.

"There were a young feller once. Joe Shaw he was called. My father had a little shop in Settle. Only a small place down a side street. He sold vegetables, but we considered ourselves a cut above them what only had a market stall. Well, Joe Shaw only had a market stall, and when he asked me to marry him I turned him down. I thought he weren't good enough for me." Bella's eyes watered, and her lips trembled. "I weren't good enough for him. Oh, as soon as I'd done it, I knew I'd made a mistake, but I had too much pride to tell him, and when he married that Jane Armitage I couldn't bear to go on living in same town, so I took this job up here to get away. You know, Mistress Leah used to say, 'The flowers of all our tomorrows are in the seeds of today.' There'll be no flowers for me, Mistress Damaris."

"There will be flowers for you, Bella. In fact, you would have had some today if I had not left them by the lake."

"You shouldn't have!" Bella exclaimed, appearing both pleased and embarrassed. "Oh dear, the men will be wanting a bite of supper. I feel that helpless lying here."

"I'll cook something."

"That's kind of you. You'll find potatoes in a chest in cellar. I put them down there when storeroom was full up. You'll need to take a candle with you."

I left Bella and entered the kitchen, and to my astonishment all that remained of the trout was the head and backbone. I stared in amazement; then I saw the culprit. It was a young black cat; thin, with beautiful green eyes, calmly washing its paws before the fire.

"You wicked cat!" I exclaimed. "How dare you eat my trout!"

She winked at me with her lovely eyes, then, stretching herself out on the floor, she placed her two paws above her head and slept.

I wondered if it was Leah's cat. She was very fond of

them, and used to keep several at a time, much to father's annoyance. He could not abide them.

Gradually I became conscious of the thundering of horses' hooves, and, feeling alarmed, I hurried across to the dining room and looked through the window. Three dragoons, one leading a spare horse on a halter lead, were galloping along the moorland road to the north. I watched them curiously until they disappeared in a cloud of dust.

I returned to the kitchen, lit a candle, picked up a basket, and cautiously opened the cellar door at the end of the room.

The steps led me down into a deep darkness, the air cold and damp, and a draft from somewhere caused the yellow flame to flicker. I reached the bottom step and shone the candle around the cellar. There was a well in the center, with a stone wall about three feet high surrounding it, obviously only used when the yard well ran dry. The wooden chest of potatoes lay by a wall. I opened it and placed half a dozen large potatoes into my basket and closed the lid.

As I was about to leave I thought I heard the sound of hammering coming from the other side of the far wall. I paused to listen, but I could hear no further sounds. Perhaps it was my imagination.

Feeling puzzled, I climbed the cellar steps. As I entered the kitchen, a strange young man with red hair was standing by the window with his back to me. He wore the loose, sleeveless leather jacket that was common in these parts.

He turned as he heard my step. I managed to stifle a gasp, for he had been branded on the cheek with the letter *R!* It was apparently done recently, for the flesh was still

red and raw.

"I'm Jack Reddihough," he said, smiling, but the smile was insolent, and he looked at me as one looks at a tavern wench.

"Well, I must say I admire Seth's taste. What have you done with Leah? Chased her away; or do the two of you share him?"

It was one of the rare instances when I lost my temper, and I threw the basket of potatoes at him. He ducked as the door opened behind him, and the basket hit Seth Paslew in the chest, the potatoes scattering at his feet.

"This is a fine way to greet me," he said, and to my relief he laughed as he bent down and picked up the basket.

"I wasn't expecting you back so soon," I stammered. "You said you wouldn't be back until late tonight."

"My business was concluded quicker than I expected," he replied, putting the basket on the table. "Well, Jack, what have you been doing to upset Mistress Damaris?"

"I didn't mean to upset her; honest I didn't." His manner was servile. "It was just a bit of fun!"

"What did you say?"

"I thought she was your fancy woman."

Seth Paslew threw back his head and laughed.

"Mistress Damaris cannot bear the sight of me. Isn't that so?"

I could bear no more, and ran from the kitchen, up to my room, and bolted the door. I flung myself down upon the little bed, thinking how much I hated Seth Paslew and his detestable friend. The carving on the cupboard ceiling caught my eye. It was an interlocking design; each piece fitted into the next in a never-ending pattern. My life was such a pattern, and I was trapped in it.

Then I turned my gaze toward the window. The evening sunlight was casting a golden sheen on the old stone slates of the stable, and a blackbird perched on the cornerstone and started to sing. Its thrilling notes soothed my troubled mind, and as I listened a calmness washed over me like the waves of the sea.

I had to make Bella's herbal tea. I rose from the bed, walked across to the little silver mirror, and combed my hair. As for the Paslews, they could make their own supper.

There was no one in the kitchen. I made the herbal tea and took it up to Bella. She must have heard the scene in the kitchen, but she said nothing, and I left her drowsing on her pillow.

It was hunger that made me do it—cooking supper for the Paslews. I unhooked a ham joint from the overhead beam, found a sharp knife and cut a few thick slices, then put them in a frying pan and set it on the fire.

As I prepared the meal I found myself thinking about Christian Malloughby. I had found a good friend in him, and this comforted me. I thanked providence for my good fortune. Then a frightening thought possessed me. Did he suspect Seth Paslew of murdering his brother? And if Seth Paslew had murdered one, why not another? Had he murdered Leah? No, these were mad thoughts, and yet I wondered.

When the food was ready I took it into the dining parlor and we sat down to eat.

Seth Paslew pushed his plate away, went across to the sideboard and poured himself a generous measure of brandy, then returned to the table. I thought he seemed edgy and ill-at-ease, and I wondered if he, too, had seen the dragoons riding across the moor. He drank too much. Was it to keep his nerve?

"Jack Reddihough called to see about the shearing tomorrow." Seth Paslew was speaking to his father. "He's a good, quick worker. He'll be alright."

I thought of the brand mark on Jack Reddihough's face and it sickened me. What had he done to deserve such a terrible punishment?

Then Seth Paslew turned his attention to me. His face took on a stern expression, and his voice was harsh.

"I've told you there's a meeting here tonight. They'll be coming as soon as it gets dark. Go up to your room and bolt your door. I don't want to see you again until morning."

I took the supper dishes into the kitchen and put them on the table. I felt uneasy. What kind of meeting was it where I was banished to my room?

I went upstairs and bolted the door, as Seth Paslew had instructed, undressed and climbed into bed. The sky was the pearl gray of dusk and the clouds were black.

I lay there wishing I was back in my own room at Calverley, where the gardens swept down to the river. On warm summer evenings, Leah and I used to walk along the riverbank, where touch-me-not grew, thick and shoulder high on each side of the bridle path. It had been like walking through a forest of pink blossom.

Was Seth Paslew a smuggler—on the grand scale? How else could one explain the fine clothes, the thoroughbred horse, the good wines and brandy. Probably those coming to the meeting were also smugglers. They would arrive with wagons or pack horses laden with the contraband, which would be stored here— in the cellar, or the empty rooms I had discovered on the

65

first night. Then the goods would be dispersed by Seth Paslew and his father throughout the area. I lay there, tense and afraid, a pulse beating in my head.

Then I heard them—the men of the moors. They came silently and secretly, one by one, in the dark. I crouched at the window, staring into the darkened yard below. They did not bring their lanterns for fear of being seen. They spoke in low voices and entered the house. There were no wagons or pack horses, and this puzzled me.

After a while there were no more footsteps beneath my window, and I knew their meeting had begun. Only the floorboards separated me from the room below, and I could hear the buzz of their voices.

I lay down on the bed, praying for sleep that would not come. Then suddenly I heard the cat crying. It was a muffled cry, coming from a long way off. The crying became more and more demanding. Eventually, I was obliged to get up. I lit the candle and unbolted the door. The corridor was empty and the crying seemed to be coming from a room near the oval window.

I tiptoed nervously down the corridor, and stopped outside the room. Yes, the crying was coming from there. Slowly, I turned the handle and looked in. The poor thing was standing just inside the door. I picked her up and stroked her.

"That was a silly thing to do, getting yourself shut up in here," I whispered.

I glanced idly round the room. It was a sad room, smelling of damp and decay. Clothes were scattered about the floor, but Seth Paslew's finely embroidered bottle-green waistcoat had been carefully placed over the back of a chair. There was a heavily carved bed against one wall. It had once been a fine four poster; now the bed curtains hung in shreds. I walked across and touched them. Yes, they had once been fine velvet, a long time ago, when the Paslews had owned their own land, and been proud and prosperous, and mixed with the gentry. Seth Paslew's saddlebag was lying on the bedside table, empty now. I wondered what had made it so bulky when he set off that afternoon.

I left the room with the cat in my arms, closing the door firmly behind me. I felt somewhat guilty that I had been prying further into the private affairs of Seth Paslew, but the cat's insistent crying had driven me there. I tiptoed down the stairs. As I passed the door of the front parlor I could see a light shining beneath it, and I heard the low murmur of voices. I hurried into the kitchen and opened the back door.

"Silly puss," I said as I set her down on the doorstep.

As I tiptoed past the closed door of the front parlor I heard Seth Paslew's voice: "I think it would be a good idea if we lie low for a while until this has blown over."

There were cries of dismay.

Then Seth Paslew's angry voice shouted: "Would you prefer to dance on the end of a rope?"

Then, to my horror, the door started to open. I blew out the candle and pressed myself as hard as I could against the wall of the dark passage.

CHAPTER 6

"I could have sworn I heard someone in the passage."

I recognized the voice of Harry the carrier.

"You're getting the jitters, Harry," someone shouted. "You're as weak as a woman."

"Shut the door!"

It was the angry voice of Seth Paslew.

The door was closed.

My legs were shaking and I felt faint. Stealing down the dark passage, my heart thumping against my ribs, I was afraid I might pass out before I reached my room. If I was discovered here in this passage, what punishment might these desperate men perpetrate? I opened the stairs door slowly, my heart missing a beat as it creaked. Then, closing it carefully behind me, I crept up the stairs.

Reaching the little room, I bolted the door very firmly and crawled into bed. From downstairs the din increased. I could hear the sound of breaking glass, and the thud of a heavy piece of furniture being overturned. Then the men poured out of the house into the back yard. Someone was being chased. There was a scuffle, then a pitiful cry. I put the blanket over my head as a feeling of nausea swept over me.

After a while everything became strangely quiet outside. My curiosity overcame me and I peered nervously through the window. To my horror, a body was hanging from the apple tree, and in the moonlight I could see it was Harry the carrier!

He had been kind to me yesterday; now his life was finished. What had he done to arouse such terrible vengeance in these men? As I fell asleep I wondered if there was a wife and children somewhere on the moor waiting for a man who would never return.

I awoke next morning to the sound of sheep bleating beneath my window. I sat up and looked out. The back yard was full of sheep, and when I looked at the apple tree I noticed that the body of Harry the carrier was gone. It was just as if the murder had never occurred, and the whole terrible incident had been a nightmare.

I dressed quickly and went downstairs. The sight of the upturned settle and broken glass upon the floor of the parlor showed me it had been no nightmare. This was real, and the evil in the house seemed to crowd in on me.

On entering the kitchen I was surprised to see Bella bent over the fire stirring porridge in a big black cooking pot. The cat sat next to her, purring contentedly. Here at least was normality.

"Bella, you shouldn't have got up. You're not well enough."

Bella straightened up and smiled weakly.

"I'm feeling a bit better," she said. "I'm happy working. Besides, them two will be getting another housekeeper if I'm up there too long."

She spooned some of the porridge into a bowl for me and set it on the table. Then she sat down opposite me,

and I looked into her face. I wondered if she knew about the hanging. If she did, she gave no sign of it.

"They're shearing today," she said, pouring tea from a large brown pot. "They work up a big appetite when they're shearing, and they'll be wanting a good supper tonight. 'Tisn't fair to leave it all to you, especially when you're not used to it.

"I'll boil a big piece of mutton, and get some haverbread made," she said thoughtfully, but as she picked up her spoon to stir her tea her hand trembled.

"You're not fit to be up!" I cried.

"I'm not going back to that bed," she exclaimed. "I do feel a bit weak, but as day goes on I'll mend. I got so miserable yesterday thinking about things . . ."

"You mean Joe Shaw?" I said softly.

She nodded, wiping a tear from her eye.

"Well, no use crying over spilt milk."

Seth Paslew had told me to go when Bella was better. I could not go yet; she was far from well.

"Have you had the herbal tea?"

"Aaye, I had it first thing."

I poured her another cup of tea. I was getting very fond of Bella.

"Did the black cat belong to Leah?"

She nodded.

"She were fond of that cat. Went everywhere with her. When she went for walk on moor it used to follow her."

I finished eating and rose from the table.

"I must help you, Bella. Tell me what I can do?"

"Oh I can't, Mistress Damaris," Bella replied, embarrassed. "You're not a servant like me."

"No, I insist." I said.

"Alright then," she relented, smiling. "Will you get

71

some ale from storeroom, and take it out to the men. They're in sheepfold. It's too hot to work in barn. There's four of them. Master Seth's helping them."

This was a chore I did not care to do, but I had to help Bella. I poured the ale into four tankards, set them on a tray and left the house, stepping carefully through the milling sheep to the fold at the back of the barn. How comical and woebegone they looked as they passed me, naked of their wool.

I leaned over the wall of the sheepfold. The sun was already hot and Seth Paslew, the old man, Jack Reddihough, and a young lad worked stripped to the waist, their bodies glistening with sweat.

Each man sat on a stool, holding a sheep between his legs; while the left hand held the animal still, the right hand worked the shears. Up the belly, round the shoulders; then he turned the sheep around and completed the operation, and the fleece came off in one piece.

The young lad picked up the fleece, added it to the pile in the corner of the fold, then, opening the gate, pushed the shorn sheep out. Here the sheep dog took over, herding the sheep around to the backyard.

As soon as the men saw me they came across and took the ale. I did not look at Seth Paslew, but kept my eyes down. Here was a murderer—a brutal man who knew no mercy. Did he suspect that I had been in the passage last night? I could not be sure.

The men drank greedily. Jack Reddihough had a soured expression upon his face, and I thought the old man looked ill. His face was gray.

"When we've finished, we'll take them down to the new pastures," Seth Paslew called. There was an eagerness in his voice I had not heard before. "That should fatten them up."

What did he mean—the new pastures? As the sheep passed me I noticed how thin they were. There was precious little nourishment on the moor. Seth Paslew probably always got a poor price for them at the sheep fair, I thought.

In the front parlor of the house, the smell of stale brandy and ale was overpowering. I hurried across the room and opened the windows, letting the fresh moorland air fill the room.

The parlor was an appalling sight. Broken glass lay in pools of spilled ale, and by the upturned settle one of the Delft plates lay in fragments on the floor. I picked the pieces up carefully and laid them on the dresser. The men who came last night were little more than animals, and I could feel nothing but repulsion for them. And what a wretched existence! If you were caught, it meant the gallows. If you were not, you lived in fear of being caught.

I found a broom and swept up the broken glass. As I swept, I thought about my peaceful, orderly home in Calverley. It was another life!

When I returned to the kitchen, Bella was mixing oatmeal and warm milk in a large earthenware bowl.

"You should have left the parlor," she said as I walked in. "I could have done it while the haverbread was baking."

I watched her shape the dough into two large rounds. Then she put them on the backstone, and while we waited for the bread to brown, I found myself thinking about Seth Paslew. He was the strangest man I had ever met.

"Who taught Mr. Paslew to read, Bella?"

73

He had not learned to read Shakespeare and Milton at the dame school.

"It were an old school master in village," she replied. "He took a liking to Master Seth. Oh, he had such a thirst for learning, did master, and he were bright and quick. It broke his heart when old man said he had to go to your father's forge to learn iron work. He should have been a schoolmaster or a lawyer, or summat like that. But he never had a chance—cos there were no money."

Normally, I would pity such a man—frustrated in his ambitions, forced to do menial work. But not when he had committed murder!

When the bread was baked to a delicious-looking golden brown, Bella took it off the backstone.

"That's as good haverbread as you'll find anywhere," she said, beaming. "Now, why don't you go for a nice walk, Mistress Damaris?"

I thought it a good idea, for the heat from the kitchen fire made the room unpleasantly hot. I put on a bonnet with a wide straw brim, and tied the ribbon under my chin.

"I'm really sorry you've not seen your sister. If she's not at home, where is she? I hope nothing's happened to her."

I left the house wondering if I would ever see Leah again. The sun glared down and the air was hot and still as I set off across the moor, following the zig zagging sheep track. The peace of the moor had a soothing effect on me. One sheep track petered out and another one began. The moor seemed to go on forever, dipping and rising like a sea. In the distance, a heat haze had gathered. I was a lone figure in a green-blue landscape.

Suddenly my foot stumbled on something in the

heather. I bent down to examine it.

It was a green shoe!

It had been there a long time, judging by the poor condition of the leather. I picked it up. It was a woman's shoe. Elegant, with a pointed toe; the heel was a high French one. Not the sort of shoe a moorland woman would wear. Then I felt a tingling of excitement within me. I had seen this shoe before!

It was Leah's shoe, and inside was the shoemaker's name: "John Nichols, Calverley." Leah always wore green. Bessie, our housekeeper, used to say, "You'll die in green, Leah." Die! I must not think like that.

What was Leah doing walking across the moor in high French heels? I at least had had the foresight to bring flat shoes with me. Didn't she have time to change into shoes more suitable for walking? And why had she not picked up the shoe when she lost it?

I looked around the moor. There was no one in sight. Where was Leah now? Was she in danger?

Just ahead of me, on the left, lay a farm, built on three sides of a yard. Beyond it, the moor sloped down to a small valley—a gill, they call it in these parts—where a group of cottages clustered at a crossroads beneath the shadow of a steep fell.

I reached the farm and paused, wondering what to do. Perhaps the farmer had seen Leah the night she ran away. It was a poor-looking place, the windows of the farmhouse being small and dark. The barn on the left looked empty. On the right, there was a stable with an outside flight of steps leading up to a small green door, and where the steps adjoined the wall, ferns grew.

As I stood, wondering, the farmhouse door opened and a woman appeared. She was knitting in that strange tossing motion, with the knitting sheath at her waist. Did everyone on this moor knit? Her apron was none too clean, and her dark hair hung untidily about her face. It was a young face grown old too soon. A face that had known only hardship. Two small girls clung tearfully at her skirt.

"What do you want?" she demanded, her expression hard as she walked toward me across the farmyard, knitting all the while.

Then one of the little girls ran across the uneven cobblestones and fell, bursting into a howl of weeping. Instantly, the woman was at her side. She picked up the little girl in her arms, her face suddenly full of softness and love.

"There, there, my little bairn. You're not bleeding. It's just a bit of dirt and will wash off in beck."

She moved toward the house with her other child following. Then, suddenly remembering me, she stopped and turned around.

"Were you wanting summat, mistress?"

Then I saw her eyes go to the green shoe in my hand.

"What you got there?" she demanded sharply.

"I found it on the moor."

"There's nobody here." Her voice was frightened.

She knew I was looking for Leah!

The sun was low in the sky as I entered the backyard of Wath Riding, now empty of sheep, and the house was deathly quiet as I opened the kitchen door. Bella was nowhere to be seen. There was a pot of mutton simmering over the fire, and a freshly baked apple pie cooled on the table. But where was Bella? I ran up the stairs to her room. She was lying on her bed, asleep. When she heard my footsteps on the wooden floor she opened her eyes.

77

"Bella, it was too early for you to resume your household duties. Now you stay here until you're better."

I went downstairs and made her herbal tea and brought it up to her.

"That sleep done me a lot of good," she said, handing me back the cup and lying back on the pillow.

"Bella, I wonder what caused your illness? Did you eat the same food as we did that night?"

"Yes, mistress, like I always do—except of course I didn't have no wine. I had ale instead."

"What makes you think the old man poisoned you?"

"I don't trust him. He's not been same since his wife died. Sometimes he does queer things."

"Such as?"

"Talking to her in his room. I can hear him sometimes. Gives me the creeps, it does. And he lays out her clothes . . . shoes, stockings, gown and cap. Once he got angry with me because I didn't set her a place at table."

So that's who it was for!

"But that isn't sufficient reason to try to poison you, Bella."

"There's something else. You see, I once told him I were quitting. I'd had enough."

"What do you mean, Bella?" I asked softly.

Bella did not answer, turning her face away. I had no wish to upset her, but I still pulled Leah's shoe from my pocket.

"I have something to show you," I said.

She turned her face toward me, looking astonished.

"That's Mistress Leah's shoe! Where did you find it?"

"On the moor. Who lives at the farm near the little valley?"

"You mean going down to Hawksgill? That's Thwaites place. I don't have much to do with them. She's not very friendly. Why do you ask?"

"Nothing. Just curious."

I felt it best to keep my suspicions to myself.

Seth Paslew and the old man were still at the new pastures, so I ate alone that evening. I felt pleased I had found Leah's shoe—it seemed to bring her closer to me. Christian said he would help me, and I decided I would ask him to accompany me to Thwaites' farm as soon as possible. I felt sure Mistress Thwaites knew something about Leah.

The house was filled with a sweet stillness, and I could feel hope bubbling up within me. Outside, the light was fading fast from a pale lilac sky. I saw two black silhouettes on the skyline. Seth Paslew and the old man were returning, and my spirits dropped like a stone.

I hastily finished the meal and went into the front parlor, closing the windows. All trace of the stale alcohol had gone, and the only evidence of last night's activities was the overturned settle. I made an attempt to move it, but it would not budge.

I sat down on the rocking chair and wondered what Bella was afraid to tell me. Was she concealing the smuggling activities of Seth Paslew? I dreaded meeting him.

I found myself staring at a curious hole cut into the stone slab that lay across the top of the fireplace. Suddenly, Seth Paslew's voice startled me, and his hand touched my shoulder. It was big and powerful. It could kill a man. I felt a shiver run through me.

"After Christianity came, they still clung to the old gods on this moor. One of them looks through that hole.

79

He is watching over you, seeing that you do not come to harm."

"Is there a chance harm may come to me?" I asked.

He laughed. A relaxed, confident sort of laugh.

"Not if you keep out of my way!"

You killed a man last night, I wanted to say, but all I said was, "Is the flock on the new pastures now?"

"Yes, and it's only the beginning. Ten acres and they're mine."

I was perplexed. At roughly £10 per acre, he needed £100. How had he acquired such a large sum? Until last summer he had been working for my father, who paid small wages.

"Where exactly are the new pastures?"

"At the foot of Wath Cliff, in that little valley."

I shuddered.

"What's the matter?" he asked.

"The scene of so many deaths. Isn't that where Widd Malloughby was killed?"

His expression hardened.

"What do you know about Widd Malloughby?"

There was something about his tone that frightened me.

"I know nothing except that his body was found at the foot of Wath Cliff."

There was a long silence. The evening shadows played upon his face, and I wondered what dark thoughts he was thinking.

"You'll go in the morning." His voice was commanding.

CHAPTER 7

I did not expect civilities from Seth Paslew. He was bent and twisted as the tree that grew on the moor.

Upstairs in the little room I climbed wearily into bed. I needed time. Time to investigate Leah's disappearance. Time to help Christian solve the mystery of his brother's death. But Seth Paslew was master here, and I had to obey.

I fell into a troubled sleep. When I awoke, rain was beating against the little window. Suddenly I knew I had to go to Winterburn Hall and see Christian. He would know what to do. In the maelstrom of Wath Riding, I saw Christian as a rock to whom I could cling.

Dressing quickly, I put on my dark traveling gown. It would be a wet and dismal walk to Winterburn Hall, but it had to be done. Packing my few belongings into a small bag, I thought of Bella. I had to say goodbye to her. Taking my cloak from behind the door, I slipped it around my shoulders and gave the little room one last look. There was no feeling of regret, rather a sense of many things left unfinished.

Opening the stairs door, I saw Seth Paslew standing in

the entrance to the front parlor.

"You're wise to rise early," he said. "It's a long walk to Settle."

"It will do me no harm," I replied. Then the fact that I was leaving gave me the courage to speak my mind. "I shall not be sorry to leave this place. I came to see my sister, and to find that she has disappeared has caused me great anxiety."

He did not answer. His face was a mask. There was so much he could tell me, but he had chosen silence.

As I pulled on my gloves, the dining parlor door was flung open, and the old man rushed into the passage.

"Revenue man!" he panted, pointing a trembling finger at the front parlor window. "That's second time I've seen that devil in past week."

"For God's sake, calm yourself." Seth Paslew's voice was irritable, but I could see he was scared, for a nerve twitched in his cheek.

Through the window I saw a dark figure on horseback. He had stopped his horse at the point where the muddy track led to the farm, and he appeared to be considering his next move. His black tricorne was pulled well down over his brow, and his dark great coat was buttoned up to the chin to protect him from the rain. Then, his mind made up, he turned his horse and trotted along the track to the gate.

"He'll search the place, Seth," said the old man fearfully, his hands trembling violently. "He's that new feller they've sent up from London."

There was fear on Seth Paslew's face. I had not thought him capable of such an emotion. He turned quickly to me, his eyes narrowing speculatively.

"Will you delay your departure, Mistress Nunroyd,

and carry out an errand for me?"

Here was my chance!

"What is it?" I asked quickly.

He hurried across to the dresser where a square tobacco box stood. I had seen the old man take tobacco from it the night I arrived. Now, to my surprise, he brought from it a small leather bag.

"There isn't much time. I'll tell you on the way to the stable. Quick. Follow me!"

I followed him across the dining parlor and into the kitchen.

"It's very simple. All you have to do is meet a man in the Old Cock Inn. It's just on the outskirts as you approach Settle. You can't miss it. His name is Shaw. Joe Shaw. Say I sent you."

We were now in the backyard and crossing to the stable.

"All you have to do is give him this bag of money and in return he will give you some papers. Guard them carefully; they're valuable. Bring them straight back to me."

He opened the stable door and brought out Roxanna. To my surprise, she was already saddled.

"I intended going myself. I would have let you ride pillion with me. I wouldn't let a pretty thing like you walk all that way."

I gave him a look of contempt. He handed me the small leather bag, and I placed it in the deep pocket of my cloak. Then, mounting Roxanna, I gave her a nudge with my heels, and we trotted out of the yard and around the house. The revenue man was dismounting at the front door, and I caught a quick glimpse of a gray, steely face.

When I reached the road I turned Roxanna left toward

the village, and pulled the hood of my cloak down as far as it would go. The rain had turned to a fine drizzle, and the moor was covered in a thick white mist, muffling all sounds and creating a deathlike hush.

I wondered if I had made the right decision, but it was too late now to ponder. I was on my way to meeting a man called Joe Shaw. Bella was going to marry a man by that name. Could it be the same man?

It was about ten miles to Settle, so I relaxed into a comfortable position, and let Roxanna go at a steady trot. I did not like the moor that morning. The mist gave it an eerie, ghostlike atmosphere, making one think of spirits from another world. Suddenly, my ear caught the sound of galloping hooves. Was the revenue man following me? Had he found something at Wath Riding, and was I now under suspicion? I gave Roxanna a touch of the whip and she went like the wind. As we passed the twisted tree, for a brief, terrifying moment, I thought I saw poor Jinny's mother hanging from the bough.

Soon the road started to run downhill, and Wath Cliff came into view, magnificent and sinister in the mist. I slowed Roxanna down, and when I saw the friendly cottages of the village at the bottom of the hill, and the mist lifting, I was no longer afraid. Who ever had been following me had seemingly given up the chase.

Passing the Quaker Meeting House, and the Woolpack Inn, where through the window a cheerful fire blazed, my spirits rose. The rain stopped, and a watery sun bravely tried to pierce the mist that still hung in the atmosphere. Beyond the village, the scenery changed to flat pastoral country, and an occasional coach or gig passed me on the road.

I began to feel more cheerful, comforting myself with

84

the thought that perhaps I was wrong in interpreting events so sinisterly. Revenue men call at houses to collect taxes, and Seth Paslew had asked me to perform an errand for him.

Castleberg Fell now loomed ahead of me, with the market town of Settle nestling in its shadow. Rounding a bend in the road, I approached the Old Cock Inn. It appeared to be a converted cottage, a poor place, the habitat of farm laborers and itinerant journeymen; the sort of place ignored by the stagecoaches as not respectable enough.

A young stable lad took charge of Roxanna, and I entered the inn, feeling a little apprehensive, for surely no respectable woman would enter here. It was a dark, dismal place. The stone floor was bare and the uneven, plastered walls were painted brown.

Opening a door on the left, I found myself in a barroom. There was a stuffy smell of stale ale and tobacco smoke. Arranged against the walls were rough wooden benches, and on one side stood a crude sort of bar with casks of ale and pewter tankards. A solitary man was seated on a bench by the window.

I approached him. He was a short man, with a pot belly, flamboyantly dressed in a light green coat with black buttons, a yellow neckcloth. Below his coat yellow stockings showed.

"I'm looking for Joe Shaw," I said nervously.

"I'm him," he replied without smiling.

His eyes were small and shifty. I did not like the look of him.

"Seth Paslew has sent me."

He looked surprised.

"So he sends a lass instead."

His voice was sardonic and he invited me to sit down.

"Have you brought the money?" he asked sharply.

I brought out the leather bag and gave it to him.

"I understand you will give me some papers."

"Why couldn't Seth come himself?" he asked, unbuttoning his coat.

Some instinct told me to be discreet with this man.

"He was delayed," I answered.

From his inside pocket he brought out a sheaf of papers and placed them on the table. Then he picked up the leather bag and loosened the draw strings.

"I won't count it now. Seth wouldn't be such a fool as to cheat me. Here, give him these." He handed me the papers. I took a quick glance at them before folding them up. They appeared to be I.O.U.s.

"I'm a dealer in bills," he said, looking at me intently. "Give them to Seth; and to keep it businesslike, sign this."

He pushed a paper before me.

"What is this?" I asked.

"Only a receipt. I want your signature."

I was not going to sign my name on any paper. Then I would be truly implicated in this business.

"Isn't the money good enough? You don't need a receipt."

"You're a sharp one," he said, looking at me through half-closed eyelids. "I haven't seen you before."

"I'm Seth Paslew's sister-in-law."

"That's a new one."

I began to feel uncomfortable and rose to my feet.

"I must be going, Mr. Shaw."

"It's the horsefair today. I suppose you'll be going?"

"I'd forgotten all about it," I exclaimed.

"Well, look after your brass. They're a thieving lot in Settle. Oh, and I saw you riding up on a fine looking horse. Don't take that in market square. They'll have that sold afore you can say Jack Robinson. We're not called Yorkshire tykes for nothing!"

"Thank you for your advice, Mr. Shaw."

I turned to go.

"Oh, by the way, is Bella still up at Wath Riding?"

I hesitated a moment before answering.

"Yes, she is." I replied.

I left the inn with a feeling of relief, and walked quickly up the busy road toward the market square. There was no accounting for taste. Bella was too good for him, I thought.

The market square was packed with horses. The crowd was noisy and boisterous, many of whom had come from the surrounding counties, and as far away as Scotland. The horse fair at Settle was famous. I watched with interest while the owners paraded their horses up and down before prospective customers. There were hunters, brooding mares, geldings, yearlings, shire horses for ploughing, Cleveland bays for pack-horse work, smart-looking pairs for carriage work, and ponies to pull gigs and for children to ride upon.

Ragged urchins fought in the mud, and an old beggar playing a flute piped an old country air as he wandered through the crowd. Stalls had been set up where saddles, harness, boots, Yorkshire woven cloth, and cheeses of the dales could be purchased.

Wath Riding seemed far away.

Beneath the arched colonade of the shambles, a long stone building on one side of the square, hot pies and other tasty items to tempt one's appetite were for sale. I bought a pie, and munched it unself-consciously beneath the arches, watching the crowd.

My attention was caught by a flashy horse dealer trying to pass off a seedy looking animal by extolling its extraordinary qualities. An unkempt youth in the crowd shouted insolently at him: "That one's ready for knacker's yard, mister."

The horse dealer looked at the boy with withering contempt.

"I'll give you half a guinea for it," the youth shouted.

"I'll have you know you could never afford the price I want for this magnificent animal!"

The youth, undismayed, pushed a shy country woman forward.

"I'll have you know our Nelly here 'as got more money in her apron pocket when she's mucking spreading than you'll ever see!"

The crowd roared; the horse dealer shook his fist, and the youth ran off into the crowd.

It was a long time since I had felt so happy. Strolling through the fair, I saw the prettiest bay filly I had ever seen. Her coat was like satin, and her eyes were soft and gentle. I stopped before her, and looked at her longingly.

"Twenty guineas," said the owner.

I shook my head.

"I can't buy her," I said sadly. "I have only a few guineas in my pocket."

The owner turned his attention to a richly dressed elderly gentleman. I thought I had seen him somewhere before, but could not remember where. I walked away.

Suddenly there was a commotion. I looked across the milling mass of people and horses to see a dragoon on horseback pushing his way through the crowd.

"Make way!" he called.

The crowd parted and let him through. He rode across to the steps of the town hall and dismounted, then proceeded to take down a notice, now hanging in shreds, and nailed the new notice in its place. A crowd gathered round, full of curiosity. I pushed my way through as best I could and, raising myself on tiptoe, managed to read the notice:

COINERS
COMMITTED TO
YORK CASTLE

ON SUSPICION OF CLIPPING, FILING, EDGING, AND DIMINISHING THE GOLD COIN OF THIS KINGDOM.

ON WEDNESDAY EVENING THE 16TH MAY WAS COMMITTED TO YORK CASTLE JOHN GREENHOW OF HALIFAX ON SUSPICION OF DIMINISHING THREE GUINEAS AND ONE TWENTY-SEVEN SHILLING PIECE OF PORTUGAL GOLD. AFTER HE WAS SEIZED THERE WERE FOUND IN HIS POCKETS A PAIR OF SCISSORS AND AN INSTRUMENT FOR MILLING THE EDGES OF GOLD PIECES.

IT IS ALSO CONFIDENTLY ASSERTED THAT THERE HAVE BEEN ABOVE ONE HUNDRED PERSONS INFORMED ON, AND THAT THERE ARE NOW WARRANTS OUT AGAINST THEIR ARREST.

I moved away from the crowd, filled with a strange anxiety. Why had Seth Paslew been so desperate to get that bag of money out of the house before the revenue man entered? What was he afraid of? And I did not trust Joe Shaw. That shifty-eyed little man smelled of deceit. Respectable business transactions do not take place in places like the Old Cock Inn. I was a fool to have become involved.

I left the square and walked slowly up a steep lane. The noises and smells of the horse fair gradually receded, the higher I climbed. Small cottages clustered on each side of the lane. In another month their neat gardens would be a blaze of color. Children played while their mothers hung the clothes on the lines that zig-zagged overhead.

Soon I left the cottages behind, and the lane petered out into a footpath. I was on the lower slopes of Castleberg Fell. Here the wind was gusty and tore at my cloak, billowing it out like a cloud. Higher up sheep grazed, moving like small white dots on the fellside.

Ahead of me was an ancient oak tree growing by the side of the path, and there was a dark shape hanging from the bough. At first I was puzzled, for I could not make out what it was. Then as I drew nearer, I stopped, horrified, as I realized what it was.

It was the body of a man, clad in irons!

My blood froze within me. This was the second body I had seen in the last few days, but the horror was in no way diminished. There was a terrible grating sound as the wind swung the body to and fro. It was like a death knell. It caught at my raw nerves and I felt I wanted to scream. Someone had put an old felt hat upon his head and his eyes looked upward to the heaven he would never attain.

A woman came along the path at that moment, a basket

on her head. She paused and regarded the body coldly.

"Who was he?" I asked in a strained voice.

"He were a coiner," she answered. "And it'll be a grand day when they catch the ringleader and hang him, too." Then she put her basket down and, putting her hand in her apron pocket, she brought out a guinea.

"That's all the money I have in the world, and no shop in Settle will touch it. Do you know why? It's been clipped—do you see, it's smaller than it should be. I could starve for all them coiners care."

Then she picked up her basket and walked on.

CHAPTER 8

I walked down the hill into Settle, my suspicions deepening. Was Seth Paslew a coiner? I had never seen a clipped coin in my life, and knew nothing about the wretched trade, but from the tone of the woman on the hill the coiners were bitterly hated. By clipping coins they were cheating honest people of their money. On the other hand, Seth Paslew and his associates could be smugglers, as I originally suspected. Smuggling, I argued to myself, meant that poor people had a chance to drink tea or wine or even brandy.

As I arrived in the market square, the horsefair was drawing to a close. I bought some oranges from a stall to give to Jinny and Bella, then made my way to the Old Cock Inn. There I mounted Roxanna, and joined the busy road out of Settle. There were carriages and farm wagons crowded with passengers, and horseback riders leading their new purchases on halter reins.

I became pensive as I trotted along; Seth Paslew and Leah filling my thoughts. I was considering my best course of action when the decision was made for me. Not far from Wath village a fine carriage overtook me, and I recognized the occupant as the elderly gentleman who had been interested in the bay filly. I saw him look sharply at me, then he tapped his driver on the back with his gold-topped cane, and as his carriage came to a halt, he waved me to stop.

I rode up to the carriage door, wondering who he was.

"Am I right in thinking you are Mistress Damaris Nunroyd, daughter of Samuel Nunroyd of Calverley?"

I told him I was, noticing his claret coat richly trimmed with embroidered silk, and his neckcloth decorated with the finest lace. The door of his carriage bore his coat-of-arms—a ram and a white rose on a blue shield. Where had I seen that before?

"Thought it was. Never forget a face! I met you at your father's house last year. Do you remember? Came to see him about a business proposition."

I remembered him now. He was Sir Matthew Malloughby. There had been a possibility of him buying a half share in the forge, but owing to some disagreement, the deal had fallen through.

"I like to dabble, you know. But what an extraordinary coincidence, meeting like this! Look, we're just at the turning for Winterburn Hall. Do me the honor of taking tea with me, Mistress Nunroyd. It would give an old man a lot of pleasure."

How could I refuse such a charming request? It would make a pleasant interlude in a somewhat unpleasant day, and, besides, I wanted to see Christian. I could see the roof of the hall rising like a citadel above the trees to the left.

Trotting behind at a respectful distance, I followed the carriage up the drive. A wood grew thickly on each side so that I could see nothing of his land. After about half a mile the trees started to thin out and the hall came into view.

It was an impressive mansion of gray stone, with numerous latticed windows set in large square Tudor bays. A flight of steps led up to a great iron-studded door, over which was displayed the Malloughby coat-of-arms.

The carriage stopped at the foot of the steps and a groom appeared.

"Put the carriage away, Rob," said Sir Matthew as the groom helped him out of the carriage. "I won't be using it again today. And stable Mistress Nunroyd's horse until she is ready to leave."

I followed him up the steps, and the great door was opened by a butler in dark blue livery.

"I've brought a visitor for tea, Beckwith. Tell the kitchen."

I was conscious of Beckwith's curious stare. No doubt he was not accustomed to guests arriving in such a wind-blown condition. My cloak was crumpled and my hair tangled from the wind on Castleberg Fell.

We walked into a large room with a high, raftered ceiling.

"Used to be the great hall in Medieval times," Sir Matthew remarked.

The floor was paved in black and white marble, upon which were scattered Persian rugs. Large, gold-framed portraits of solemn-looking ancestors hung on the oak-paneled walls. Arranged against the walls were handsome cabinets and chests of drawers, some inlaid with designs of birds and flowers. On a table by the window, the afternoon sunshine danced on a figurine of a Greek nymph.

We sat down on a sofa of crimson velvet. Sir Matthew

had that smooth confidence and ease of manner that comes from wealth and position. His silver-gray hair was tied back with a wide black silk ribbon. He was very old, but his face still bore traces of his handsome earlier days.

"You wouldn't think I was eighty-five, would you, my dear?" He looked at me expectantly.

"You look much younger, Sir Matthew," I replied. "You could pass for sixty with ease."

"Flattery won't get you anywhere," he said, obviously pleased, his blue eyes twinkling.

"I still ride every morning, only drink champagne, and I'm in bed every night by ten. Now, you can't do better than that. I'll tell you my little secret—a calm mind is the most precious possession you can have. I never worry about a thing. Now, tell me what you were doing alone on the Settle road."

How could I tell him that the unexpected arrival of a revenue man had caused Seth Paslew to ask me to meet his business associate.

"I had just been to the horse fair," I answered. It was partly true. "I do believe I saw you there. You were interested in that beautiful bay filly."

"I bought her. One of my grooms is bringing her back. Yes, she's a beauty, but not much of a pedigree. However, I'm still puzzled. Where are you staying?"

"Wath Riding."

"The Paslews' place?" His forehead creased into a frown. I would have to tell him.

"I came to see my sister. She married Seth Paslew. He used to work for my father at the forge . . ."

"What was your father doing to allow your sister to marry one of his iron workers?" he interrupted. Then, without giving me a chance to reply, he continued: "I don't know what's the matter with young people today. In my day, people kept to their class. Anyway, the private affairs of my tenants are their own concern. So long as they pay their rent. I can't say they keep their property in good repair, because according to my agent the barn at Wath Riding has needed repairs these past two years. How is your father?"

"He's very well, thank you."

I was glad of a change of subject.

"I admire men like your father. Iron masters, mine owners, ship builders. The way I see it, the future wealth of this country is in their hands."

A manservant entered, bearing a silver tray on which lay delicate bone china tea cups and plates of thin bread and butter. There was also a bottle of champagne and a glass.

"I take champagne, if you don't mind, my dear."

As the manservant poured out the champagne, I heard the sound of a door opening, and Christian walked quickly across the room. I thought he looked pleased to see me.

"Christian! I'd like you to meet Damaris Nunroyd— my great nephew, newly arrived from the New World. Damaris' father is a business friend of mine. Met her on the Settle road, unescorted if you please."

Christian bowed low over my hand.

"This is indeed a pleasure. We have actually met, uncle."

"You don't waste much time, Christian," Sir Matthew laughed. "Got an eye for a pretty face, like your old uncle, eh?"

"May I sit next to you, Damaris?"

"Certainly."

Christian sat next to me on the sofa and I handed him a cup of tea. The look of sorrow had gone from his eyes, and his refined features were relaxed and smiling. Here, I felt, was a kind man, who would never knowingly harm anyone. We sipped our tea and Sir Matthew drank his champagne, chatting all the while on matters of little consequence.

"How did you get on at the horse fair, uncle?" Christian asked.

"Bought a filly. Prettiest thing you ever saw, Christian. You must go to the stable and take a look at her. Tell me what you think. You won't find a horse like that in Virginia," he teased.

"Don't you be so sure, uncle," laughed Christian. You'd be surprised what we have in Virginia. Would you mind if I smoked, Damaris?"

"Not at all."

Christian brought out his pipe and lit it.

"I presume that is tobacco from your plantation," I said.

"It certainly is."

"Tell me about Virginia."

"Well, I've told you our place is on the James River," said Christian puffing at his pipe. "I reckon our plantation is the biggest in the country. We have a fine red brick house, and a rose garden. I can still smell those roses," he added nostagically.

"You're homesick already, Christian," commented Sir Matthew. "And the pity is you've come on a wild goose chase. Of course I'm delighted to see you, but there were no mysterious circumstances surrounding poor Widd's death. Remember, we had the evidence of his depression."

"Who sat on the bench?" I asked innocently.

"I did of course," said Sir Matthew. "It's very difficult to keep law and order today," he continued. "The number of poachers brought before me is dreadful. Poor fellows, they're starving to death some of them. The bad harvests of recent years account for that. Rise in prices, unemployment; no wonder they turn to breaking the law . . ."

"And turn to coining?" I added.

"Why do you say that?" asked Sir Matthew.

"They've hanged a coiner on Castleberg Fell," I said.

"Coiners are the scourge of the country," thundered Sir Matthew. "The sooner they are all hanged the better. Bankruptcies are constantly coming before the bench. The poor wretches, usually trades people in a small way, find they have only clipped money in their possession, and cannot pay their taxes. There is no alternative for them but the debtors' prison. Often they die there. Yes, the coiners have a lot to answer for. They are responsible for a great deal of misery."

I had no idea Sir Matthew was so passionately against the coiners. I was sorry I had mentioned it.

"How long are you staying at Wath Riding?" continued Sir Matthew.

"I'm not sure. You see, my sister is missing and no one knows where she is. It's most odd. Then the housekeeper was taken ill and I stayed to look after her. I shall probably leave tomorrow."

I gave Christian a careful look.

"You must indeed be worried about your sister, but I think the best thing for you is to return home. There is nothing you can do, and your parents must be worrying about you."

"I'm sure you're right. Well, I must be going," I said reluctantly. "The tea was delicious." I rose to my feet. "You have some fine portraits here, Sir Matthew," I commented, looking around.

"Are you interested in paintings?"

"Yes, I am."

"Well, you must come upstairs and I'll show you my studio. I dabble a bit in oils."

"No visitor can get away without seeing uncle's paintings," laughed Christian as we crossed the room.

"I'll see you at the stables before you go, Damaris," called Christian as he left the room.

Sir Matthew and I climbed the staircase at the end of the great hall, and at the first floor we entered a small room at the front of the house. This was Sir Matthew's studio. There was a large window to give him maximum light, and stacked against the walls were his canvasses. I walked from picture to picture, viewing them carefully. He was an accomplished artist, and had captured a strange, mystical quality in his paintings of the moors and fells.

"You should exhibit in London," I remarked.

"That's very kind of you, Damaris," he answered.

"I believe it was your brother who emigrated to America," I asked.

"Yes," replied Sir Matthew. "Josiah hated Yorkshire. He hated the mists, the rain, and that damp cold that penetrates to the very bone."

"And you love it. I can see it from your paintings."

"Yes I do. I'd never leave here."

On an easel by the window was a large painting. I walked across and viewed it with interest. It was a half-finished picture of Wath Cliff.

"I'll finish that one day," he remarked. "I can't quite get it right."

We descended the stairs and entered the great hall.

"When I die," said Sir Matthew, "all this will go to Christian."

"He's very fortunate," I remarked.

"There's something I'd like to show you in the library—that is, if you are interested in antiquities."

I assured him I was and followed him into a room that led off the great hall.

"This is the library," said Sir Matthew. "Used to be the kitchen before it was converted. Hard to believe, isn't it."

The walls were lined with books from floor to ceiling. There must have been several thousand there, and on the floor was a crimson and green Turkish carpet. There was a walnut writing cabinet richly decorated with crimson flowers, and intricately carved high-back chairs with velvet seats. An occasional table held the figure of a bronzed satyr, but what interested me most of all was a fragile glass dish in a display cabinet. It was enameled in faded pink and blue, but there was something strange about it. It was crudely made, and seemed out of place amidst the luxury of the library.

"That is what I wanted to show you," said Sir Matthew proudly, walking up to the cabinet. "That bowl is known as 'The Luck of Winterburn.' When that breaks, our luck breaks with it."

"What is the story?" I asked, intrigued.

"It was the time of the Wars of the Roses. After a battle up here in the north, a shepherd found the king wandering exhausted on the fells, and he brought him to Winterburn Hall. The Lady Margaret nursed him back to health, and to show his gratitude, he gave her that bowl."

We left the house by a side door and crossed a paved area where peacocks strutted to the stable block.

"I will leave you now in the capable hands of my nephew. Do come again, Damaris. Give my regards to your parents. And take my advice—go home. Wath Riding is no place for you, my dear."

He took my hand and I bobbed him a small curtsey.

What a delightful old man, I thought as I watched him return to the house. Then a groom led a fine black stallion and Roxanna out of one of the stable entrances with Christian following.

"I thought I'd ride with you as far as the moor," he said. "That is, if you care for my company."

"Christian, you are my only friend," I said as I mounted Roxanna.

"What were you doing at the horse fair?" he asked as we trotted down the drive.

I told him the whole story.

"Could I have a look at those bills?" he asked when I had finished.

We stopped our horses by the roadside and I brought the bills from my pocket.

"They seem to be mainly I.O.U.s on merchants in Bradford and Leeds," he said, handing them back to me.

"Who was this man you bought them from?"

"A dealer in bills called Joe Shaw."

"I should think it's a risky business," he commented. "Seth Paslew has no guarantee he will get the money from these men."

We rode in silence for a while.

"Damaris," said Christian. "There are rumors of coiners on Wath Moor."

We had left the village and were riding up the hill.

"It's well organized so there must be a leader," he continued.

"How do you know?"

"Last night I went to the Woolpack Inn. There was an old man there who had had quite a bit to drink. He started talking. He was upset because his wife's brother had gone bankrupt. A tradesman in a small way. His takings had included a good deal of clipped money, and when he came to pay his taxes, the revenue man would not accept it. He's been taken to York Castle for nonpayment of taxes.

"The old man told me how the coiners clip gold off a coin, then file the edge to make it look as though it hasn't been touched. When they have sufficient clippings, these are melted down and made into new coins. It's big business."

Christian stopped his horse and brought from his pocket a handful of coins.

"That's a Portuguese moidore, this is a Louis D'or, this is a Spanish pistole, and this is an English guinea. The coiners clip as much as five shillings worth of gold from each coin. I wonder if the trouble arises from having foreign currency in general usage in this country. People are not familiar with alien coins, so that when they do see one they do not realize that it is not the correct size. Just a theory of mine."

I could offer no opinion on the matter, the coins I handled being few.

"These isolated places are so far from the law, they feel safe," continued Christian. "And no constable is going to ride twenty miles over rough country on the strength of a rumor. More than that, there is a state of apathy. No one will take the initiative and do something; some are too frightened."

"Do you think Widd knew about the coiners," I asked after a while.

"I'm sure he did," answered Christian.

"I tried to talk to Seth Paslew about him last night," I said, "but he would not discuss the matter."

"I think it's high time I came to see Mr. Seth Paslew," said Christian grimly.

"Take care, Christian. They hanged a man two nights ago."

"Who was the man?"

"The carrier. He gave me a lift the day I arrived."

"If we could find out why they hanged him, we'll learn a lot more about Seth Paslew. By the way, any news of your sister?"

"Yes," I replied eagerly. "I found her shoe on the moor yesterday. It was near Thwaites farm. I saw Mistress Thwaites and I feel sure she knows something; in fact I think Leah's been there."

We reached the top of the hill and Wath Moor stretched before us. We stopped our horses.

"We ought to go to this farm," said Christian quietly. "Could you think of some excuse and meet me tonight?"

I nodded.

"I'll think of something. Meet me on the moorland road just past Wath Riding at sunset."

Christian's hand touched mine. It was as light as a bird's wing. He's shy of women, I thought. Then he turned his horse and was gone. I gave Roxanna a touch with my heels and set off at a brisk canter along the lonely moorland road.

CHAPTER 9

It was a pleasant ride. The late afternoon was warm and sunny, and when the road dropped down into the hollow and Wath Riding came into view, for one brief moment it was nothing more than a peaceful domestic scene, with the smoke spiraling from the kitchen chimney, and the distant barking of the sheep dog.

Then I saw him! The tall, powerful figure of Seth Paslew leaning against the gate, clearly awaiting my return. My mood of quiet contentment vanished as I cantered across the heather to meet him. I should not have lingered so long at Winterburn Hall.

"Where have you been?" he shouted as I pulled Roxanna to a halt. "I've been waiting these past two hours."

"I went to the horsefair," I said, dismounting. "You need not have worried. I have your bills safely in my pocket."

Seth Paslew opened the gate and scowled at me as I passed through.

"Let's have them," he said roughly.

I handed them to him, and he took them without

a word.

"You might have the courtesy to thank me," I said coldly, but either he had not heard me, or he had no desire to thank me, for he walked away and entered the house.

The old man appeared, and, taking the reins from my hand, he led Roxanna away to the stable muttering she had been ridden too hard and he needed her tomorrow to take the fleeces into Settle.

I followed Seth Paslew into the house, and found him seated on the window seat in the front parlor, deep in thought.

"What did Joe have to say?" he said as I walked in.

"He wanted to know why you hadn't gone yourself."

"And what did you say?"

"I told him nothing."

"You did right. I don't want my private business blabbered about Settle."

These were words of praise indeed from Seth Paslew. Was I actually rising in his estimation? I sat down on the window seat and looked at the bare stone floor, and the few simple pieces of furniture. The contrast between Winterburn Hall and Wath Riding could not be greater, yet strangely enough I did not mind.

"Anything else?"

"He wanted me to sign a receipt. I refused."

He put the I.O.U.s in his breeches' pocket.

"You spent a mighty long time at the horsefair."

I did not like the suspicion in his voice. I had just done this man a favor, and he did not trust me.

"I met Sir Matthew Malloughby on the way home. He invited me to tea at the hall, and I accepted."

I waited for an exclamation of sarcasm, or even

pleasant surprise, but instead his face darkened with anger.

"Keep away from Sir Matthew," he shouted. "You hear me? I won't have you going there."

I was equally angry now.

"What right have you to tell me what I must do?"

Suddenly he grasped me viciously by the wrists.

"You're hurting me!" I cried.

"While you're in this house, you obey me."

"Let me go!" I cried.

Then, like a gale dying down, his mood changed. He let go my wrists and his face softened.

"I have no right to be angry with you. You did well today."

Then he stood up, walked across to the cupboard, and poured himself a brandy.

I rubbed my chaffed wrists. His changes of mood never ceased to surprise me, but something must have upset him today. It must have been the visit of the revenue man.

"What did the revenue man want?" I asked as innocently as I could.

"They say a new broom sweeps clean." There was sarcasm in his voice. "Well, he won't find anything here."

Did the revenue man suspect Seth Paslew of being a coiner, I wondered. Then I thought of the dragoons I had seen galloping along the moorland road on Sunday. Had they arrested a coiner?

"Anything new in Settle?" Seth Paslew asked.

"A coiner has been hanged on Castleberg Fell."

I watched him carefully as he poured another brandy, but his expression was noncommittal.

"Settle is becoming a bit uncomfortable these days," he replied. "Remember the old saying 'From hull, hell and Halifax, the good Lord deliver us'—they should include Settle in that."

He smiled sardonically at me.

"You mean the 'Thieves' Litany.' Well, you have no cause to worry, Mr. Paslew."

He put his empty glass on the dresser.

"You drink too much," I remarked.

"I'll thank you to mind your own business," he snapped. "If I want to drink myself to death, that is my affair."

It was a waste of time talking to him.

"I bought oranges at the fair for Jinny and Bella. I'll take some along to Jinny tonight."

He did not appear interested.

Later that evening, when supper was finished, I went to the kitchen to see Bella. There was a healthy glow about her face, and she was energetically scouring pans. Bella was her old self again.

"I'm glad to see you're feeling better, Bella, Here's a little present for you." I put the oranges on the table.

Her face lit up at the sight of them.

"Eh, thank you Mistress Damaris. There's nowt I like better than oranges." She dropped them into her voluminous apron pocket. "It's just like Christmas being given oranges," she said, her face beaming with pleasurable anticipation.

As I left the house the sun was low in the sky, casting a warm amber light across the moor. I did not have far to go before I saw Christian waiting for me by the roadside.

"Christian!" I shouted, and started to run.

"I thought you were never coming," he said as I drew near. "Any trouble at Wath Riding?"

"No," I answered, as Christian helped me mount his horse. "Except Seth Paslew does not want me to visit Winterburn Hall."

"I'm not surprised," laughed Christian. "Home of the local magistrate."

We set off at a quick trot and soon reached Thwaites' farm, built on the lonely hillside that sloped down to Hawksgill. There was no one in sight, and all that could be heard was the gentle movement of a cow in the barn, and from the top half of the stable door a shaggy pony watched us.

We walked up to the farmhouse door, and Christian knocked. There was no answer. He knocked again, and still no one came. I was beginning to feel the journey had been wasted when there was a shuffling sound behind the door and the sound of the bolt being drawn back. Then Mistress Thwaites' unhappy face stared into ours.

"What do you want?" she demanded ungraciously.

"I—I wondered if you could help me?" I asked hesitantly.

"Help you about what?" Then she looked hard at me. "Haven't I seen you before? Here, I don't want no more trouble. I've had enough what with my Will being taken away."

Her lip trembled. So that was who the dragoons were after!

"I'm sorry about your husband, Mistress Thwaites. I had no idea he had been arrested."

"It were all that carrier's fault. Blabbing his mouth to get the reward money. The nasty, sneaking rat. Hanging were too good for him."

"It will be difficult for you to run the farm single-handed," commented Christian, looking around.

"I'll manage," she said, tightening her thin lips. "I had to manage before when Will had the accident with his leg."

So the man with the wooden leg I had seen the night I had arrived was Will Thwaites. It was all fitting in.

"And what do you want with me?"

"My name is Damaris Nunroyd, and this gentleman is Mr. Christian Malloughby."

"Squire's nephew." Her voice had a sneer in it.

"That's right," he said. "This lady's sister has vanished from Wath Riding, and she wondered if you would help her."

"How can I help? I know nothing about her sister."

"That's not true," I said. "You saw me yesterday when I found Leah's shoe. I think you know something, and you're afraid to tell me."

The woman was now clearly agitated.

"Has Seth Paslew sent you? I want no trouble from him."

"He knows nothing of this visit, I assure you. Is my sister still here? I beg of you. Please help me find her. I'm desperately worried about her."

It must have been the look of pain in my face, of supplication in my voice, for the mood of angry defiance softened. I was not surprised, for I knew there was compassion beneath that cold exterior.

"She were here," she said in a subdued voice.

"When was that?"

"Before Christmas. November. Yes, it were November. She come very late one night."

"What do you remember of that night?"

110

Mistress Thwaites thought for a moment before she answered.

"Cow were calving. It were getting on for midnight, and Will says he'd go down to Hawksgill for help. Just as he gets onto moor your sister come running along like a wild thing, she almost bump into him in dark. So Will asks her where she's off to at that time of night. She seemed very upset and asked for bed for night. Wouldn't tell him nothing. I put her in room over stable. Poor lass, she must have been unhappy to run away. She went early next morning."

"Which way did she go?"

"I saw her running down to Hawksgill."

"Could I see the room?"

Taking a lantern from inside the passage, she led us across the yard and up the steps to the little green door. Then, flinging it open, she shone the lantern inside.

"You see, it's clean. We had a farmhand live here once, when we could afford it."

There was a small truckle bed beneath the solitary window. The rest of the room was bare, and from below came the sharp odor of animal smells. I walked across the room. My instincts had been right. Leah had been here. Poor Leah. How desperate she must have been. But what had made her run away?

I glanced through the little window. The moon was shining brightly on the cottages in the valley below, and the fell behind was a black, sinister shadow. Then I spotted a strange object on the hillside. It was a standing stone about five feet high. In the moonlight it seemed to take on a human appearance. There was something hauntingly sad about it, as if the head was tilted up in humble supplication.

"What is that?" I asked Mistress Thwaites, pointing to the stone.

"That's Stoney Meg," she replied. "Happened a long time ago. She had an unlawful love affair with her brother-in-law. One night the two lovers decided to run away. They'd only got as far as that hillside when God's wrath was smitten upon her, and He turned her into stone. Let that be a warning to all lustful sinners."

Her words sent a chill through me, as though a cold hand had clutched me.

"Thank you for being so helpful, Mistress Thwaites."

We left the stable room, Mistress Thwaites leading the way, her lantern casting a pale yellow light across the farmyard.

"My sister would only have one shoe," I remarked.

"I gave her an old pair of my boots. Better than having her feet cut on them stones."

Such a woman would have difficulty in finding an old pair of boots—boots were wore until they fell apart. This poor woman had given Leah her own boots. Her generosity overwhelmed me. I took a guinea from my pocket.

"Please take this, Mistress Thwaites."

"I won't take no money from you," she said proudly.

"Take it for your children's sake," I beseeched her.

After a little coaxing she relented, and pocketed the money.

"I wouldn't have taken it if Will had been here."

"Mistress Thwaites, why were you so frightened yesterday when you realized I was looking for Leah?"

"She made me promise that if any one come inquiring after her to tell them nothing. She were in trouble."

"What kind of trouble?"

112

"I don't know, but she were very upset way she were going on. I told you she were here because I could see today you didn't mean her no harm, you only wanted to help her."

We bid each other farewell, and I climbed up behind Christian on his stallion.

We trotted out of the farmyard and into the darkness of Wath Moor. What kind of trouble was Leah in? If only I could find her.

"I suppose you're longing to go down to Hawksgill," said Christian, looking back at me over his shoulder. "And ask at the cottages if anyone has seen your sister."

"Yes," I replied, "but it's too late to go there now."

We rode in silence for a while before Christian spoke again.

"You're a good friend, Damaris."

"Why do you say that?"

"You're restoring my faith in women," he replied.

"Can you tell me about it?" I asked in a soft voice.

"It was just about the time I was leaving America. I was deceived by someone. After that, I thought all women were selfish and shallow."

"You're very kind, Christian," I said softly.

We had now reached Jinny's cottage.

"Will you please stop here, Christian," I said. "I want to see Jinny for a moment."

Christian waited at the gate while I walked up Jinny's garden path. The door was half opened, and in the dim light of the interior I could see her spinning by the fire, the soft whirr, whirr, filling the room.

"Why, Mistress Nunroyd," she exclaimed, pausing in her work as I entered. "I hope Bella isn't ill again?"

"No. I'm not here on account of sickness. I have

113

brought you a few oranges from the horsefair."

I laid them on the table and their warm color glowed in the firelight.

"That's right kind of you," she said, touching them tenderly with her old gnarled hands. "'Tis a long time since I've had a gift from the horsefair."

Then she looked at me shrewdly.

"Your sister will never come back to Wath Riding."

She spoke with such conviction I felt certain she knew where Leah was.

"You must tell me where Leah is, Jinny."

I could not keep the desperate note from my voice.

"Have they told you I have the second sight?"

"No," I said in almost a whisper, feeling somewhat disquieted.

"Follow the ley."

"The ley?"

She nodded. "The track runs straight."

Then she sat in her chair by the fire and closed her eyes.

"Jinny."

There was no answer. It was if a door had closed in her mind.

I walked out of the cottage.

"You look as though you've had bad news," said Christian as I joined him at the gate. "Did the old woman have anything to tell you about your sister?"

"She told me to follow the ley," I replied as he helped me mount. "I don't know what a ley is."

"I'm afraid I can't help you, Damaris, not being a Yorkshireman. Perhaps if you asked people who live around here they may be able to help you."

We rode for a while in silence, each busy with our own

114

thoughts. Then Christian spoke: "Damaris, I've been here four days and discovered nothing further about Widd's death. It's been a waste of time coming to this country, except of course for meeting you. But I have learned about the crime he uncovered."

"Are you suspicious of anyone?"

"Yes, and I think you know who I mean."

"Seth Paslew?" I said in a low voice.

"Yes. And I'm going to see that gentleman tonight, and ask him a few pertinent questions. I shall also ask him to clip a coin. If he does it and before my eyes, I've got him. You see, before I can get him arrested I must have evidence."

We were now approaching Wath Riding. The farm lay in darkness save for a solitary light in the window of the front parlor. I felt apprehensive and afraid. When we reached the gate I dismounted and opened it and Christian's horse clattered into the front yard.

"It's best if I go in by the kitchen door. Good luck."

I left Christian knocking at the front door and hurried as quickly as I could to the back. Bella was still up. She was pouring honey into a big cauldron of warm water.

"I was just making a drop of mead," she said as I walked in. "You can't get it off that smuggler fellow. Anyway, he only sells that foreign rubbish." She spoke with disgust.

As she stirred the honey and water the atmosphere was filled with a delicious fragrance. I almost envied her. A good woman, a simple life, no problems or worries, except of course turning down Joe Shaw's offer of marriage twenty years ago. And if she only knew it, it had

115

been a lucky escape.

I bid her goodnight and went upstairs to the little room that was now almost as familiar as my own. The front parlor being directly beneath the room, I could hear the men's voices quite clearly through the chinks in the floor boards. I stood still, listening, my heart beating fast, as I heard Seth Paslew speaking.

"Widd came here often. We used to go shooting together. I tell you I know nothing about his death. He did come here the last night he was seen alive. His horse had cast a shoe. That's the horse Roxanna that's in the stable now. I told him I couldn't shoe her until morning and he said he had to return home—he would go on foot, taking the short cut along the top of Wath Cliff. I told him he was a fool to go that way. It was dangerous. He wouldn't listen to me."

Then I heard Christian speak: "Widd could be as obstinate as a mule when he liked. So he took the short cut and was never seen alive again."

"That's right. My father showed him the way."

There was a short pause.

"And where's your father now?"

"He's gone to bed. He's not feeling very well."

"Will you tell your father I'd like to speak to him sometime? I'd just like to hear in his own words how my brother was killed."

"Have a drink before you go."

Seth Paslew was being the polite host.

I undressed and crept into bed. The conversation turned to more mundane matters such as sheep rearing and tobacco planting, and as I grew sleepy the voices became blurred. Then suddenly I was raised from the edge of sleep by Christian's voice, loud and clear:

116

"Will you clip this Portuguese moidore for me, Mr. Paslew?"

I waited with bated breath for Seth Paslew's answer.

CHAPTER 10

"What makes you think I'm a coiner, Mr. Malloughby?"

"I heard a rumor in the village."

"Don't listen to rumors."

Had my suspicions been wrong? What could this new development mean? The revenue man had obviously found nothing. Perhaps Seth Paslew was, after all, just an innocent sheep farmer. He did a little blacksmith work on the side, and with his savings had invested in the purchase of I.O.U.s. That still did not account for the new pastures he had just acquired. I felt confused.

I heard Christian leave the house, and then, not long after, the back door closed and Seth Paslew's footsteps sounded across the back yard. I knelt at the window and watched him hurrying past the barn. Then he disappeared around the corner. He carried what appeared to be an empty saddlebag.

His business at the lake cottage, for that was where I presumed he was going, must have taken a long time, for I did not hear him return, and when I awoke the morning sun was streaming through the little window.

I got up and dressed. I had no excuse for staying any longer, I thought as I went down the stairs and opened the stairs door. Perhaps today was my last day.

The passage was empty and very quiet. I went into the dining parlor, then the front parlor. They were deserted, peaceful, the sunshine casting golden pools of light onto the stone floors.

It was going to be a hot day.

Then I heard a noise. It was a very faint, thin sound, almost like a child crying. I went into the passage and stood still, listening, feeling perplexed. At the end of the passage was the closed stairs door, and to the right the two empty rooms I had noticed on the day of my arrival.

I walked down the passage and stopped outside the second empty room. The sound seemed to be coming from there. I opened the door and stepped into the room.

It was Leah's cat crying.

But the sound was muffled, as if the poor thing was trapped in some enclosed place. Beams of diffused sunlight shone through the dusty window into the empty room. The furnishings had no doubt been sold long ago to pay the Paslew debts. Dead flies from summers long passed littered the floor, and cobwebs festooned the cornices.

Standing in the center of the room, I listened intently. The cat's crying seemed to be coming from behind an alcove which was built into the wall on the left of the fireplace. It was small, about three feet across and about seven feet high, filled with shelves which at one time would have held books or the mistress's treasured china.

How on earth had the cat got behind there? I could see no opening, no broken section of wall. Perhaps there was a way in through the fireplace. I knelt down in the hearth

119

and ran my fingers along the stone work inside the fireplace. It was quite firm.

I was indeed puzzled. There must be some way in, I thought, as the pitiful crying continued. I put my hands up to the shelves and shook them, and, to my astonishment, the back of the alcove opened inward, and out of the dark space stepped the cat. It walked up to me, rubbing itself against my legs.

"You silly cat," I scolded, picking her up and stroking her silky black fur. "That's the second time you've got yourself locked in somewhere."

The cat struggled to be free and I let her go. She ran swiftly from the room and out into the passage.

The yawning black hole behind the alcove tempted me. I could not resist it. But first I needed a light. I hurried down the passage to the kitchen. Thankfully, Bella was not yet up. Quickly lighting a candle from the fire, I hurried back to the empty room and stepped gingerly into the black cavity.

In the light of the candle a flight of stone steps led downward, and to my surprise the air was not cold and damp as I had expected. I closed the alcove door and placed my foot on the first step. My hand trembled as I held the candle high to give myself as much light as possible. I started to walk slowly down the steps.

There were nine in all, and at the bottom of the steps there ran a short passage, which turned sharply, and I found myself in a small cellar. There was a fire burning in a low-arched open hearth, casting a pale orange glow onto the whitewashed walls, and showing in soft relief the spiders' webs and patches of soot that had gathered in the dimples of the uneven surface of the walls. Overhead, the ceiling was curiously arched, with hooks hanging from it.

Several small pieces of furniture were arranged against the walls. There was a blacksmith's anvil near the hearth, a pair of bellows, and, on a stone table in the center of the room, were a variety of tools, including several pairs of large scissors, files, a hammer, and what looked like a number of golden disks. I picked them up curiously. They were blank on both sides, and looked as though they were made of gold.

Near the disks were three steel blocks. I could not think what their purpose could be. One was oblong with a hollow center, and the other two were also oblong in shape but solid, with a small circular design engraved on each side.

I held the candle close to the engraved designs. I had seen similar steel engravings somewhere before, perhaps at a printing house in Leeds where father had once taken me on a visit. He had said they were called die blocks.

Suddenly my blood froze in my veins as I heard the sound of footsteps coming down the stone steps.

I was trapped!

Looking frantically around the cellar for a hiding place, my eye alighted upon a wooden chest just beyond the stone table. I ran to it and lifted the lid. It was empty save for a few empty sacks lying in the bottom. Blowing out the candle I quickly scrambled inside and lowered the lid. My heart was beating so loud I feared that whoever it was might hear.

The footsteps drew nearer. They were heavy masculine steps. It had to be Seth Paslew. The old man walked with a shuffle, and Bella's steps were quick and light. Then I heard the bellows being worked, and after that there was such a long silence. I wondered if I was alone.

I raised the lid of the chest half an inch. I was not

alone. Seth Paslew was standing before the fire, his back toward me. Gaining courage, I raised the lid another half inch.

Then he turned around. There was a lantern in his hand and he placed it on the table. I watched him pick up one of the blank disks and push it into the mold. Then, picking up one of the die blocks, he rammed one into the cavity on the right side, and the other die block into the left side. When he was satisfied they were in position, he picked up the hammer and hit each end of the die blocks hard. He put the hammer down and pulled each die block out of the mold. Then he put his hand into the cavity and brought out the disk, examining it in the lantern light. Picking up a file, he filed the edge smooth. When he was satisfied, he placed it on the table in the pool of light cast by the lantern. I stared like someone mesmerized.

It was a newly minted guinea!

To my horror, he looked up and appeared to be staring at me. I lowered the lid of the chest and crouched in the bottom, trembling. I felt sick, and my head was swimming.

I could almost feel his strong hands tightening around my throat, and I was floating in an empty void. I must have fainted, for I remember opening my eyes, moving my cramped limbs, and feeling that if I did not get fresh air soon I would die.

My sense of self-preservation being stronger than my fear, I raised the lid of the chest just an inch, and the fresher air of the cellar revived me.

The golden disks had now been turned into guineas and were piled up on the table. Seth Paslew was busy taking coins from his saddlebag. I could see they were old, worn coins, such as those in daily use. Picking up a pair scissors, he skillfully clipped a small section from the edge of each coin, then filed the edge smooth.

He sat on the rim of the table, working quickly, concentrating on his task in hand. The pile of clipped coins grew, and the pile of gold clippings grew. Soon he stood up and scooped the gold clippings into a leather bag, and the clipped coins into his saddle bag. Taking a key from his pocket, he walked across to a cupboard on the other side of the cellar, unlocked it, and put the saddlebag and the leather bag inside. Then, locking it up, he moved to a chest next to it and locked that up also.

I lowered the lid of the chest, my heart fluttering, a lump in my throat so large I could barely swallow. What would happen to me if he decided to lock this chest? I knew the answer: it would become my coffin. I lay there in an agony of suspense, my hands and face wet with perspiration. Then, like an answer to my prayers, I heard him leave the cellar, and my agitation subsided.

I waited a long time, not daring to leave the chest. When I was sure he would not return, I raised the lid, stepped out, and stretched my cramped legs. Oh, the relief to be out of that chest. Now to be out of this cellar.

As I walked past the table I noticed a wooden box. It was small, about fifteen inches by ten. I opened it.

It was filled with freshly minted guineas!

I dipped my hands in and let the bright coins trickle through my fingers. It was a peculiar sensation, for I had never seen so much money in my life. Then I gave a shudder and closed the box. It was death money! The penalty for his crime was to swing in irons!

I stood up and looked around. Here I was in the private mint of a coiner . . . perhaps the leader of the coiners— the man the county was seeking. Sir Matthew and

Christian would be delighted when I told them what I had discovered, and my spirits rose at the thought.

But first I had to get out of the cellar. I lit my candle at the fire and retraced my steps along the passage and up the stone stairs, breathing a sigh of relief when I reached the back of the alcove door. But on shining my candle upon the door I could discover no means to open it. There was no handle or knob. The door closed flush with the wall, and the surface was entirely smooth.

I began searching for a spring that would release the opening mechanism, running my fingers over the surface of the door, and around the edges of the wall. But the door remained closed. I put the candle on the floor and banged the wooden panels with my fists in the vain hope of accidentally touching the secret spring, but nothing happened. The door remained firmly closed.

If only I could be sure that Seth Paslew and the old man had left the house, I could shout for Bella to help me, but I could not take the risk.

I was incarcerated in this hiding place!

Picking up my candle, I walked sadly down the steps, tears of anger and frustration pricking my eyes. At least there was a fire to give me warmth and comfort in the cellar. I sat down on the little stool before the fire, a feeling of depression settling over me. I tried to think. There had to be some way out. I felt sick with apprehension.

Suddenly I remembered that cellars have air vents with iron bars over the opening. Full of hope, I walked around the cellar shining the candle along the walls, but there had either never been any vents, or they had been blocked up. I sat down by the fire, defeated.

I had been a fool. I had allowed myself to become

126

sidetracked from my original mission: the search for Leah. Christian wanted me to help him, but he did not wish me to risk my life. Seth Paslew would not allow me to remain alive. There was too much for him to lose. This freshly minted money would buy back the Paslew land he wanted so desperately, and he would eliminate any obstacle that stood in his way. I shivered before the warm fire.

There was coal on the fire!

All the other fires in the house were peat, and that was stored in the barn. Where could the coal be stored? In a cellar, and cellars have coal chutes. We had one in our own house at Calverley. A small opening in the side of the wall through which the coal was thrown.

With renewed heart I picked up my candle and stood up. There was no coal in this cellar. I walked slowly along the passage, shining my candle as I went. When I came to the steps, to my delight, I saw a small space I had not noticed before between the steps and the wall on the left side. And in that space the coal was piled up against the wall! There was no sign of any coal chute. There was no other choice but to remove the coal with my hands to find it.

I put the candle on one of the steps, and, kneeling down, started to remove the coal piece by piece.

It was the dirtiest and most unpleasant job I have ever done. I worked hard, and soon my back was aching and my hands hurt from the sharp pieces. Time and again I wanted to give up, but I would not allow myself. When I was about to give up hope I nearly shouted for joy, when after moving a particularly large piece of coal, I saw a chink of daylight.

With renewed energy I worked harder, and soon the

gap of daylight widened, and the full width of the coal chute was revealed.

I judged it to be about twenty inches wide, and about twelve inches deep. Being of a small build, I could just make it. It was a tight fit. I got my head and shoulders through the opening, then wriggled the rest of my body through. Puffing and panting and straining, at last I was out!

I found myself on the far side of the farmhouse. There was no one about, so I sat down on the grass, leaned my back against the wall, and took a short rest. The relief to be free of that cellar was indescribable.

So Seth Paslew was a coiner!

My suspicions had been right. It was like being hit between the eyes. When I first came here, I thought he was a smuggler, but I had never really been sure that it was wicked to be a smuggler. In fact, I thought there was something romantic about rowing into a quiet cove in the dead of night with a cargo of wines and brandy; or taking teams of pack horses across the little-known tracks over the fells and moors. But coining, this was different. This was stealing money from honest, hard-working people. I found it repulsive.

I had to tell Sir Matthew. He was the local magistrate, and that would put an end to this wretched business. I looked down at my gown. It was black with coal dust, and so were my hands and arms, and no doubt my face. What a scarecrow I must look. But more than that, it was evidence of where I had been.

I could not go to the well in the backyard for fear of Seth Paslew or the old man seeing me. Then I had an idea. I would wash in the lake, then return to the house and change my gown.

128

Scrambling to my feet, I hurried past the beehive wall and the apple tree, then up a grassy slope. I skirted around the top end of the sheep fold, and onto the path I normally used to go to the lake.

When I reached the top of the ridge I was hot and breathless. I could see the lake ahead of me through the trees. I set off again, and was soon running along the north shore. When I came to a clump of bushes I stopped and knelt down at the water's edge, and washed the coal grime from my face and arms and hands. It was such a pleasure to be clean again.

Then I stepped out of my shoes and peeled off my stockings. Holding my skirt high, I stepped into the water, feeling the soft sand squelching between my toes and the tiny wavelets lapping against my ankles. It was sheer delight.

Then a sudden impulse took possession of me. I looked around quickly; there was no one in sight. I unlaced my bodice and slipped out of my gown, then stepped naked into the lake!

The water was cold and invigorating. I waded out a short distance from the shore, then, tilting my head back, I dipped my long hair in the lake and washed it. All the fear and frustration of the morning melted away. I felt like a water nymph . . . a naiad, one of the Greek goddesses who presided over rivers and lakes. For a few brief, ecstatic moments my cares were forgotten, and my spirit reveled in reclaimed freedom. Then suddenly the mood was shattered for, to my intense horror, I saw a figure walking quickly toward me along the north shore.

It was Seth Paslew!

CHAPTER 11

He was walking fast, and every second the distance between us narrowed. I bent my head, my cheeks burning with shame, and when I looked up he was standing on the shore opposite me, staring as though he was seeing me for the first time. Then, for a fleeting moment, I caught a look of warm tenderness in his eyes. It was so sudden it startled me, then it was gone, and when he spoke there was sardonic humor in his voice.

"There's no need to bathe in the lake. You could have borrowed Bella's wash tub in the kitchen."

"I thought I would at least have privacy here," I answered. "I did not realize I would be spied upon."

He laughed good naturally.

"That's a risk you have to take when you strip in the open. You're going to catch a chill. You'd better come out and get dressed."

"I won't come out until you go away!"

I felt a feeling of panic. What would I do if he refused to go? But my fears were without foundation, for without another word he turned and walked away. I watched with relief his receding figure along the margin of the lake.

Then he struck out onto rugged ground to the south.

When I could no longer see him, I waded to the shore and dressed. What a disaster my bath had turned out to be; I had been so sure he only came this way at night.

Walking back along the shore I looked at the little cottage, remote and silent across the water. Was it a meeting place to receive and hand over money? I could not stand by and do nothing; I would then be contributing to the misery it brought. I thought of the poor woman I had met on Castleberg Fell.

By the time I reached the farm the hot sun had dried my hair, and the bath, despite my harrowing experience, had cooled and refreshed me. Bella was crossing the yard with a basket of eggs.

"What have you been doing to get so dirty?" she asked, amazed, looking at my blackened gown.

"It's a long story, Bella," I answered evasively.

We entered the kitchen together. There was a pot of porridge cooking on the fire, and the mead Bella had been preparing the night before was gently fermenting in a stone jar by the side of the hearth.

Bella touched my gown with her finger.

"It's like coal dust to me," she said, puzzled.

"I've been up to the lake," I said, trying to distract her attention, "Bathing."

Bella's eyebrows went up.

"Eh, you'll not catch me doing that! I'll have a bath twice a year, and that's enough for me. It's dangerous to wash too often—catch your death, you will."

I went upstairs and quickly changed into my blue linen gown. What a pity I had met Bella while still in my coal-stained gown. But I had learned one thing—Bella did not know that coal was stored in the farmhouse.

Rolling the soiled gown into a bundle, I pushed it into my bag; I was expected to leave today. Could I think of some excuse for delaying my departure? First I had to go to Winterburn Hall and tell Sir Matthew and Christian of my discovery.

In the kitchen, Bella placed a bowl of porridge before me on the table.

"I don't feel hungry, Bella. Just a cup of tea."

She looked at me sharply.

"I hope you're not sickening for summat. Bathing in the lake, indeed. I know someone from village who bathed up there, and they caught the pox and died."

"You can't catch the pox in a moorland lake, Bella."

There were butterflies in my stomach every time I thought of Seth Paslew. He was a coiner. A desperate man. A man who walked a tightrope every day of his life. A man hunted throughout the county. I pushed the porridge away. I was impatient to be gone.

"Has the old man gone into Settle?" I asked Bella as she poured the tea.

"He has that. And he were in one of his queer moods again."

"What do you mean?"

"Talking about her this morning. Said with the money he gets from fleeces he's going to buy her a new cap!"

Bella tapped her head sadly.

"He's weak up here alright."

It was the beginning of the end, and I wondered what would happen to Bella. I was positive she was not implicated in any way, and whatever happened I would stand by her.

"Bella, something is going to happen, and soon, and when it does, trust me."

I tried to sound casual and calm, and waited for Bella's outburst, but it did not come. Instead, a shrewd look came into her eyes.

"I hope you know what you doing," was all she said.

I left the house and walked up the rough track. At the point where it joined the moorland road there was a small black object lying in the grass. I caught my breath and knelt down.

It was Leah's cat, and it was dead!

There were no marks upon it of any kind, and no sign of bleeding. What had happened? It was alive and well only a few hours ago when I had let it out of the space behind the alcove. Did someone know it had led me to the secret mint and decided to kill it? I shivered at the thought. It had been such a pretty animal, happy in its freedom roaming the moor. Now its life was finished. I would bury her on my return; give her a decent little grave. She had been a good cat, and no doubt Leah had loved her.

The hot sun beat down upon me as I trudged the dry, dusty road to the village. The recent rain had brought the heather out, and now it lay, in all its purple glory, as far as the eye could see.

When the road descended to the village, the sun caught the white limestone and made it glitter, and in the grass at the roadside, celandines glowed like stars. There wasn't a breath of wind, and the only sound I could hear was the bleating of Seth Paslew's sheep down in the valley on my left.

A figure dressed in a bright green coat and yellow stockings was approaching me up the hill, and as he drew near I recognized Joe Shaw.

"Good morning, mistress," he said politely, taking off

134

his tricorne and wiping his forehead with an ancient looking pocket handkerchief. "It would be a hot day when I decide to go calling on Bella. I hope she is well?"

"She is, Mr. Shaw," I answered.

"I've been a widower these many long years. 'Tis a lonely life, and after seeing you yesterday and talking about Bella, I got to thinking, and I decided the time had come to pay her a call."

"That's very kind of you," I replied. "I'm sure she'll give you a good welcome."

"Are you going far?"

"No, I am not."

"Well, good day to you, mistress." He gave a slight bow, replaced his tricorne and continued on his way.

Joe Shaw going courting. I could not help suspecting his motives. There was something about the man that made me distrust him. Exactly what it was I could not say: just a look, a tone of voice. And why had it taken him such a long time to decide to call on Bella? Then I felt ashamed of myself. Here was a lonely widower seeking a little feminine company and I distrusted him.

I reached the village, and the sound of water rushing over the beck stones was cool and refreshing. The beck flowed through the center of the village, with terraced cottages clustered thickly on each bank. Each cottage had its own little garden brimming with flowers, and small stone-mullioned windows winked in the sunshine. Over each door was a date stone and the initials of the owner. I wondered where the kind schoolmaster who had taught Seth Paslew to read lived.

Crossing the pack-horse bridge that spanned the rushing water, I walked along the riverbank thick with daisies and ragged robin. Housewives were busy washing clothes, rubbing and beating on large flat stones, while their children played or squabbled. It was probably a holiday, I thought, for the Dame School across the road was silent and empty.

I walked a short distance along the riverbank until I came to the clapper bridge—a small footbridge of raised flat stones. Sitting myself down upon it, I contemplated the turmoil that was beginning to stir within me. For some unaccountable reason, I hesitated going to Winterburn Hall. I had been so sure it was my duty as a good citizen to report a crime I had discovered; now I wasn't sure. I kept seeing Seth Paslew standing there on the lake shore with that warm, tender look in his eyes, and it disturbed me. Also, I kept hearing Bella's voice saying, "I hope you know what you are doing." What was happening to me? Then I could hear my father's gruff Yorkshire voice: "You discovered a crime, Damaris, and failed to report it? You must be going soft in the head." Yes, that was it, I was going soft in the head.

Suddenly the peace of the village was disturbed by a horseman cantering down the deserted street. As soon as I saw it was Christian, I knew what I had to do.

I hurried across the clapper bridge and waved to him. He pulled up his horse and smiled.

"Where are you off to, Damaris?"

"I was just on my way to see you and Sir Matthew. I have some startling news, but I can't speak about it here."

I climbed up behind him, he turned his horse, and we set off at a steady trot in the direction of Winterburn Hall. Christian was my haven of peace. He turned his gentle, smiling face toward me.

"And what have you to tell me?"

"Christian, it's such a relief to talk to you. Last night I heard Seth Paslew tell you he wasn't a coiner; well, he is a coiner. This morning I saw him making guineas with my own eyes."

"What? How did this happen?"

I told him the whole story, and when I finished Christian laughed.

"So Seth Paslew has his own private mint. How convenient for him!"

We were now riding up the drive of the hall, and as we turned the bend we saw that a smart-looking carriage had been drawn up, with a coachman in livery holding the horses' heads. Christian gave an exclamation of annoyance.

"More visitors! I warrant it's another female. The news seems to have gotten around that I'm here, or uncle's doing a bit of matchmaking."

"Don't worry, Christian," I laughed. "I'm sure you can handle these Yorkshire women."

We went to the stables and dismounted. A groom appeared and took the horse away, while we entered the house by the side door and walked through to the great hall. As we expected, the visitors were chatting with Sir Matthew.

I noticed a young woman standing by the window admiring Sir Matthew's alabaster figurine. She was expensively attired in a loose-fitting robe of beige silk, with deep lace frills at the elbow. She wore long white gloves and a wide-brimmed silk hat adorned with yellow roses. But her face had a cold, sharp look, and when she spoke her voice had the same sharp coldness.

With her was a middle-aged lady, obviously her mother, also expensively attired. Sir Matthew was standing before the great hearth as we entered. I thought he looked a trifle weary, but he gave us a welcoming smile.

"Ah, Christian my boy, and Damaris. Allow me to introduce Lady Priestley, and her daughter Clarissa. They are neighbors from Monk's Hall."

Christian bowed politely over the ladies' hands, and I bobbed a small curtsy to Lady Priestley.

"Damaris' father owns Calverley Forge," said Sir Matthew, by way of introduction.

"Calverley Forge?" repeated Lady Priestley. Her tone indicated that I was not the daughter of a landowner, while Clarissa's hostile glance took in my plain linen gown.

Then Lady Priestley turned to Christian. He was, after all, the reason for their visit.

"I'm so sorry it's such short notice," she said, with a vivacious expression on her face, "but we are giving a small ball tonight, and would be delighted if you and Sir Matthew could attend. We would have sent a written invitation but we only discovered this morning you were here. I'm so sorry I can't invite you, Mistress . . ."

". . . Nunroyd," I interjected.

"Our invitation list is complete. Perhaps some other time."

There would never be another time, unless I married a landowner. Industry and commerce were of a lower social standing, unless, of course, the owners were extremely rich, and by no stretch of the imagination could one say that Calverley Iron Forge was one of the bastions of English industry.

"I'm not sure if I can come . . ." Christian spoke hesitantly.

"Of course you can, my boy," interrupted Sir Matthew. "I know it's feast day at Hawksgill, but surely you are not going to revel with the villagers tonight!"

"I insist on you coming," continued Lady Priestley. "And if you don't, I shall be most offended."

"In that case I shall come, I have no wish to offend you, Lady Priestley."

"Well, that's settled," said Clarissa with a gleam of triumph in her eyes. "I'm so pleased you can come, Mr. Malloughby. I persuaded Mama to arrange a summer ball for me. I think it will be quite delightful. It gets such a bore in the summer especially when people go away to the coast. I can name ten people right now who are in Scarborough for the horse racing. It's quite exciting. You should go sometime. The horses race along the sands.

"I thought we would have supper in the rose garden," she continued without pausing. "It will be lovely when it goes cool this evening, and perhaps you can tell me all about Virginia. I'm just dying to hear all about it. Is it true you have hundreds of Negro slaves?"

Then she turned to Sir Matthew.

"I just love your house Sir Matthew, don't you, Mama? Ours is quite new. It's in the classical style . . ."

Clarissa never stopped. Her mind butterflied from subject to subject, her sharp voice resounding throughout the great hall. I began to feel sorry for Christian, and impatient for these foolish, empty-headed women to go.

"Any news of your sister-in-law?" asked Sir Matthew.

"Not a word," Lady Priestley replied, her face hardening. "It's a year now since she disappeared. My husband says she's eccentric. I say she's mad. First she joins the Quakers. What a sight she looked walking about in those queer clothes. If she wasn't at a prayer meeting,

139

she was in her room on her knees. When she inherited that legacy, I think the money went to her head. There was this dreadful quarrel and her mind snapped. She wanted to help mankind."

Lady Priestley was highly amused.

At length she decided it was time to go, and Clarissa held out her small white hand to Sir Matthew and Christian. Then the two women swept out of the room like royal duchesses.

When their carriage disappeared down the drive, I breathed a sigh of relief.

"Charming girl, Clarissa," said Sir Matthew. "Talks a lot, but any man could put up with that with the dowry she'll get when she marries. Now, Damaris, you've been looking very serious ever since you arrived. Got something on your mind?"

"She certainly has, uncle," said Christian enthusiastically.

I sat down on the crimson velvet sofa between the two men.

"It's about one of your tenants, Seth Paslew. He's a coiner!"

I thought Sir Matthew took it calmly, considering how he had exploded the last time I mentioned coining.

"I heard the cat crying behind an alcove in an empty room at Wath Riding. The alcove was actually a secret door. I managed to open it, and it led me to a cellar which Seth Paslew had turned into a private mint!"

I then told him how I had hidden in a chest and watched him coining and clipping.

When I had finished Sir Matthew remained thoughtful for a while, stroking his chin.

"Have you told anyone of this?"

140

"No."

"You have been wise. I do not want anyone to know of this. We'll have to act very carefully. We are obviously dealing with a very dangerous man. First I will have to prepare a statement, and you will sign it. Christian can witness it. Unfortunately, I must be in court all day tomorrow. Will you come back on Friday?"

I agreed. I sat on the sofa, a glow of happiness flowing through me as Sir Matthew complimented me on my quick and speedy action.

"We need more people like you, Damaris."

When I rose to go Christian said he would take me home.

"Remember," said Sir Matthew. "Not a word of this to anyone."

I'll remember."

"See you on Friday, my dear."

He kissed my hand.

"I think I shall go up to my studio and do a little painting."

"Don't work too hard, uncle. You know the hot weather doesn't agree with you."

As Christian and I crossed to the stables, I thought I saw Beckwith at a window, looking at me thoughtfully. I wondered if he had been eavesdropping, and my momentary contentment vanished.

As we set off down the drive I thought Christian looked annoyed.

"I was thinking about those Priestley women," he said. "I thought their attitude damned insulting. Is that how the English upper classes behave? I've a good mind not to go."

"Don't upset Lady Priestley on my account, Christian," I said. "Anyway, I couldn't have gone if they had invited me. I didn't bring a ball gown to Wath Riding. One doesn't usually go to balls from a moorland farm." Then I couldn't resist teasing him. "I hope you have a wonderful evening with Clarissa."

"After my experience with women," he said bitterly, "it will be long time before I consider marriage. It was my own fault. I only looked for beauty in a woman—never beneath. You know, Damaris, I can talk to you in a way I cannot talk to other women."

It was the same at Calverley, I reflected sadly—young men confiding their problems to me. Would I never meet a man who thought of me as a lover, and not a confidante?

We entered the valley that lay before Wath Cliff.

"Christian, I think it would be wise of me to arrive at Wath Riding alone. Seth Paslew and his father must have no suspicions."

Christian stopped his horse.

"You're right, Damaris."

I dismounted.

"Thank you, Christian. I'll return through this valley and along the shores of the lake."

"I shall be thinking of you. You're now in a dangerous position, having informed on that man. Would it not be better to take lodgings at the Woolpack, or, better still, come back with me to Winterburn Hall?"

"No thank you, Christian. I'm sure I'll be alright."

"Don't forget, if you ever need my help . . ."

"I won't forget."

He pressed my hand and then quickly turned his horse and trotted away.

I walked across the road, climbed the stile, and started

clambering down the sides of the valley. To my surprise there were no sheep below me, save for four, dead, lying on their sides, their bellies bloated.

Feeling perplexed, I continued down the path. The folds in the hillside revealed two more dead sheep.

I crossed the beck by the stepping stones with Wath Cliff towering above. About a hundred feet up, a narrow ledge ran across it horizontally, and about the center grew a small hazel tree. It was a pity the tree had not saved Widd when he fell to his death.

Following the path that led up the steep, grassy slope on the opposite side of the valley, I paused when I reached the top and looked back. I was now level with the summit of the cliff, and it was a drop of several hundred feet to the valley below. The dead sheep looked like white dots on the grass. There was something about the place that chilled me; a sinister atmosphere, almost evil, seemed to hover. I hurried on.

The path led me over rough moorland ground. I passed the lake, and when I reached the top of the ridge, to my surprise, the flock was back on the moor. I wondered what had happened.

As I hurried down the slope I told myself I was not afraid of Seth Paslew, nor the old man, but when I entered the back yard and saw Bella standing at the kitchen door, an anguished expression on her face, her fingers working nervously at her apron, I was not so sure. As I approached her I heard a crash coming from within the house.

"Oh, Mistress Damaris. He's in a bad way, and he hasn't touched a drop neither."

"Who's in a bad way?"

I wasn't sure if she meant Seth Paslew or the old man.

"Master Seth. He's been like this since he brought the flock back to the moor. And what with that and Joe Shaw coming . . ."

"Where is he now?"

"In front parlor. See if you can calm him down. Happen he'll take notice of you."

She followed me through the kitchen to the front parlor. Seth Paslew was standing in the center of the room, the rocking chair shattered at his feet. His eyes were those of a madman.

It must have been Bella's confidence in me that gave me the courage to speak as I did.

"Control yourself, Mr. Paslew!"

"Control!" he exploded. "Six sheep poisoned and I've had to put the rest back on the moor, and you tell me to control myself!"

"Poisoned!" I exclaimed. "How did that happen?"

"Something growing in the new pastures."

"Didn't you see the ragwort?" ventured Bella nervously.

"There's no ragwort there."

"Happen it were one of them queer blue plants."

"I don't know what it is."

His anger was now spent and he sounded full of weariness. He sat down heavily on the settle.

"I've been cheated," he said in a low voice. "He knew the flock would be poisoned; that's why he never put any sheep there himself."

Then, becoming conscious of Bella and me staring at him, he turned and glared angrily at us.

"Go away and leave me alone!"

CHAPTER 12

Bella and I did not need a second bidding. We quickly left the room. I followed her to the kitchen and closed the door carefully behind me.

"Leave him be for a bit," Bella said wisely as she sat down at the table. "He always lets his temper get master of him, then he's sorry afterward."

"Do you know who has cheated him, Bella?" I asked, sitting down at the table with her.

Bella shook her head.

"I don't know, Mistress Damaris. There's nowt but sorrow in the world."

She gave a big sigh. There was a pile of apples on the table, and picking up a knife she started peeling and coring them. I was looking around for another knife so that I could help her when I saw a bunch of wild roses lying on top of the oatmeal chest.

"They're beautiful flowers," I commented. "Are they yours, Bella?"

"Nay, Master Seth brought them. That were first time he come in. I tell you when I saw him walking across yard with a bunch of flowers in his hand I thought he must have a touch of midsummer madness. There's note with them. I think it's for you."

Feeling bewildered, I went across to the chest and picked up the flowers. There was a small sheet of paper lying beneath them. I unfolded it and read: "To the distressed lady of the lake"

I found it hard to imagine Seth Paslew picking flowers, and particularly for me. Their petals were the palest of pink silk; their stamens gold dust, and their scent delicate and sweet.

I put the flowers back on the chest feeling strangely disturbed. Finding a knife in the table drawer I began peeling apples. A state of numbness seemed to overtake me, and I found it hard to concentrate on Bella's chatter.

"When Joe Shaw walked in this morning, it were like seeing a ghost. It set me all of a dither, I can tell you. I hadn't set eyes on him since I come to live here. That must be twenty year now. He hadn't changed all that much, a bit fatter than he used to be and his hair's turned gray. He said that after he married he went to live Skipton way. She's been dead a long time now."

"Is he courting you, Bella?"

"If he is, it's a funny way of doing it. He were asking questions about Master Seth all the time."

"What sort of questions?"

"Where does he go to? Who does he know? I tell you it were like being sat in front of a magistrate."

"How strange. Is he coming again?"

"He said he would. I'm not sure what to make of it. Where's that cat? I haven't seen it today."

"It's dead, Bella. I found it this morning near the moorland road."

"Dead!" exclaimed Bella. "Poor thing. I liked that cat.

I'll miss her—she were a good mouser. Wonder how it happened?"

Our conversation was interrupted by the sudden arrival of the farmcart lumbering into the back yard, and to my dismay the old man was swaying about in the driver's seat with a lady's cap upon his head. It was pulled down over one eye, with a lavender blue ribbon dangling about his ears. He looked grotesque. Bella tightened her lips.

"I knew he'd come back in this state. He's always same when he goes into Settle."

I watched the old man stagger down from the driver's seat, then reel into the kitchen, the smell of gin strong upon his breath. He was singing a lewd song.

Bella rose from her chair and faced him.

"You can stop singing them filthy songs in here. And what are you doing wearing a lady's cap, you old fool?"

"This cap is for the mistress," he slurred, taking it from his head and hiding it under his coat. "Sssh . . ." he said, putting his finger to his lips. "Not a word. It's going to be a surprise. Is she upstairs, Bella?"

"What's the matter with you," shouted Bella, "You know as well as I do, she's been gone these . . ."

"Hush Bella," I interrupted. "Leave him his dreams."

"Dreams is right," she replied. "That's all he knows—dreams."

The old man lurched through the kitchen, knocking over a stool that stood in his path, and stumbled into the front parlor. I heard Seth Paslew greet him with an angry remark, and the old man retorted in the same vein.

The quarreling continued. I was in no mood to listen, and, suddenly remembering the dead cat, I got up and went out to the barn where I saw a spade the night I slept there.

I dug a shallow grave; bluebells marking her last resting place. I wondered if she had been poisoned, and if that was so, had the same person tried to poison Bella?

I returned to the kitchen, finding Bella ready to serve supper. I had no stomach for food, but I decided to make a pretense of eating if only for Bella's sake. She took such pride in her cooking. I ate my supper with Bella in the kitchen.

"Six sheep poisoned," said Bella. "He can't afford to lose that many. 'Tisn't as if we could salt them down for the winter—you can't eat poisoned mutton. Poor Master Seth, he's had enough troubles in his life."

The inner turmoil I experienced at the village returned with a new ferocity. Of course I had done the right thing by informing Sir Matthew. Leah, I was certain, would not care. She had obviously been so unhappy she had run away. My father would be proud of me, yet somehow I did not feel proud of myself. My inner strength seemed to be ebbing away, and as I listened to the two men in the dining parlor arguing as to how the sheep were poisoned, I could hear the anguish in Seth Paslew's voice. I did not feel sure of anything anymore.

A dull ache started in my head, and began moving to behind my eyes. I shall go mad, I thought, if I don't get out of this house . . . mad like the old man.

"It's Feast Day down at Hawksgill," Bella's voice broke into my thoughts. "There'll be dancing tonight and merry making." Her old eyes twinkled, remembering. "The only day in the year when there's a bit of life on moor. Folks come from miles around. This afternoon there was cock fighting—can't say I care for that. Poor things, fighting to the death. Of course the excitement's the betting. Peddler Sam come by this afternoon, and he said an outsider called Golden Tiger won the big fight. There's been some money lost this afternoon, I'll warrant. Then there's fell racing. It's usually some young shepherd lad that wins that. It's easy for them; they're up and down fells every day of year, while weaving lads never leave their looms except Sundays to walk to church. I had thought of walking over myself, but I don't feel up to it. This hot weather wears me down."

I rose to my feet. Perhaps I should take Bella with me on Friday. Somehow I felt responsible for her. We would have to leave at sunrise before the Paslews were up.

"If you go, look after yourself," she warned me with a chuckle.

I left the house by the kitchen door and started walking. I wasn't sure where I was going. I just knew I had to get away from Wath Riding. The sun was going down, and all the colors were deepening, so that the moor became a purple fire, while to the west pink clouds filled the sky.

Seth Paslew haunted my thoughts. He was a coiner, following an evil trade, and I found that repulsive. But on the other hand I found his ambitions admirable, and, recalling the books that lay scattered about the front parlor he showed a refinement of mind that I had not at first appreciated. He was the most curious man I had ever met. Why was my conscience troubling me?

Soon the cool breeze on my face and the soft springy heather beneath my feet made me feel better. I passed Jinny's cottage, but there was no sign of her today. No doubt the hot day had tired her too, like Bella.

Soon I could hear the distant strains of flutes and drums floating on the breeze from Hawksgill. It was a sound that beckoned, and I quickened my steps over the rough moorland ground.

Passing Thwaites Farm I glanced across at the farmhouse, but there was no sign of Mistress Thwaites. I was not surprised, for I was sure she would not be in the mood for merry making.

Now the village lay before me, nestling in the little valley below. It was a small place, not worthy really of a feast day. There was a row of not more than eight cottages, clustered in the shadow of the fell, and a modest church, with neither tower nor steeple, and just beyond, a small parsonage. To the right Grisedale opened out, flanked by steep fells on either side.

On the green before the cottages several booths had been set up for serving ale and hot pies and gingerbread, and the five musicians that comprised Hawksgill's modest band sat in an old farmcart that had been painted blue for the occasion.

As I approached the green, Morris men were dancing lucky seven; their bells jingling, the ribbons on their sticks flying. The crowd was jovial and full of ale. They were mainly wool weavers, their living eked out by seasonal farm work—and perhaps coining, I wondered, as they passed me in the crowd!

I knew no one and on one spoke to me. Darkness fell and the moon shone down upon the little valley. The Morris men finished dancing and dispersed into the crowd. Then the flutes and drums struck up a lively country tune, and the village lads, some bold, some shy, approached the maidens of their choice and led them onto the green.

The dancing commenced, the moonlight paling the bright colors of the dancers' clothes to a misty gray, their

151

faces blanched and unreal. And as they danced I watched, in a kind of limbo.

"Damaris!" a voice whispered behind me.

I turned to find Seth Paslew, and I was not surprised. It was as if I knew he would come. As he gently took my hand, it was as if my will power left me, and I was drained of all rational thought.

We danced like figures in a dream!

There was a strange quality in the moonlight which seemed to change us from mere mortals into super- natural beings. We were no longer man and woman, but creatures bewitched. A spell had been cast upon us, and the drums seemed to be beating into our souls. All the time, those dark eyes burned into mine.

Then we were standing still, apart from the dancers, screened by trees, alone. With a fierceness that took my breath away, he took me in his arms and kissed me. I could feel his body throbbing close to mine, demanding possession, and I wanted him desperately—my desire for him made me feel weak. Then he was kissing my neck, his hand moving down to my breasts, and I felt the grass about my face as he eased me to the ground.

Suddenly cold, stark realism hit me like a blow.

He was my brother-in-law!

To love my sister's husband was a grave sin.

"No!" I cried. "It's wicked!"

I started to cry and he let me go. He lay on his back in the grass, his face in shadow.

"I love you, Damaris," he said in a quiet voice. "I've been fighting you ever since you arrived. I wanted you to go and leave me in peace. I didn't want the torment love can bring. But when I saw you at the lake this morning I knew I could fight you no longer. I'm your man."

He stood up and looked down at me, and in the moonlight I could see the suffering on his face.

"If you decide you want me, I'll be waiting at the farm," he whispered.

Then he turned and walked away, and I buried my face in the grass and sobbed. More than committing a sin, I had destroyed him!

After a while I stopped weeping. I was achieving nothing by it. I had to do something, but I could see no way out of my dilemma.

I sat up and looked around. I was in a small wood, and I could hear the music coming from the village green. I started running, stumbling over tree roots, not sure where I was going.

I came out of the trees, and ahead of me the dancers were still gyrating their patterns. Now it held no charm for me.

I found myself climbing the hill by Thwaites farm. Ahead of me, Stoney Meg seemed to be weeping in the moonlight.

It was like being deluged with cold water as the realization of what I must do flooded my mind. I had to find Leah and reunite her with her husband, and I could only pray God would help me. Then I would go to Sir Matthew and tell him it had all been a dreadful mistake. I had told lies to bring about the downfall of Seth Paslew.

I climbed down the hill, passed the dancers on the village green, passed the little church, and when I came to the parsonage I stopped. There was a welcoming light at the window, and I could see the silvered head of the parson bent over his quill at his desk.

I opened the gate, walked up the path, and knocked at the door.

154

The door was opened almost immediately by the parson himself. He was a small, elderly man, his shoulders hunched, his silver hair tied back neatly with a ribbon. His frock coat was shabby and worn almost through at the elbows, and on his feet were a pair of well-worn slippers. His lined face creased into a welcoming smile, and his eyes were gentle behind his steel-rimmed spectacles.

"What can I do for you, my child?" His voice was kind and encouraging.

"I'm Damaris Nunroyd. I'm so sorry to trouble you at this late hour, Reverend, but I am in need of help. Could you please give me shelter for the night, and then I'll be on my way."

"I never turn away a Christian soul in need. You'd better come in."

I followed him into the small entrance hall, where upon the white-washed walls hung a framed text which read "GOD IS TRUTH." As he opened a door and showed me into his front parlor he said smilingly, "My name is Butterwick. The Reverend James Butterwick."

I walked into a shabby but cheerful room. The rug before the hearth was threadbare, and the chairs were the type that were popular in Restoration times, with cane seats and elaborately carved backs. Some were in urgent need of repair where the cane seating had broken through. In the center of the room was a gate-legged table, and before the window was a desk.

What astonished me were the walls! They were covered in maps. I had never seen so many in one room before. They were of various counties of England. A few looked ancient and inaccurate, and one in particular was very colorful with the heading: "The West Riding of Yorkshyre with the most famous and fayre citie of Yorke 1610."

"I see you're interested in my maps," the parson smiled, obviously pleased at my interest. "Topography is my hobby. Maps have fascinated me ever since I was a boy. Please sit down, Mistress Nunroyd."

I sat down upon an insecure looking cane chair.

"Now, my child, what is your trouble?"

It was his gentle voice that gave me confidence, and I found myself relating to him the story of Leah's elopement with Seth Paslew, my decision to visit her, and the shock of discovering she had gone.

"Could you describe her to me?"

"She's young, has long brown hair, very slim, and usually wears green."

When I finished he remained thoughtful for a while.

"I do believe I saw her walking on the moor a long time ago. She never came to church here, but then she probably attended the church at Wath village. I only know of the Paslews. I believe they used to own most of this area at one time, but hard times come to us all.

156

Getting back to your sister, when did she leave Wath Riding?"

"Last November. She stayed the night at Thwaites Farm, and left the following morning."

"I'm sorry I can't help you, but I can give you a bed for the night."

"Thank you, Reverend. I'm very grateful to you."

"I always have a cup of hot chocolate and a turf cake before retiring. Like to join me?"

I protested, but he insisted.

"Now stay there. I'll make it. I'm not entirely helpless when my housekeeper is not here."

The old man shuffled out of the room. I had indeed been fortunate to find such goodness in one human being.

He was soon back bearing a tray of hot chocolate and turf cakes, and set them down on the gate-legged table.

"Come, sit at the table, my child. I'm sure you're hungry."

The hot chocolate was delicious and the turf cakes freshly made. My spirits started to revive.

"My housekeeper makes good cakes," said the Reverend Butterwick. "Don't you think? Pleasant girl, very hard working. She's married to Jack Reddihough."

Jack Reddihough! Was there no escaping these coiners, for I was certain Jack Reddihough was one of them.

The Reverend Butterwick continued chatting pleasantly about his parishioners, and when he mentioned the name Thwaites I pricked up my ears.

"Poor woman, she's suffered another calamity. First her husband is arrested for coining—I'm afraid he will be found guilty and hanged—and now some of her sheep have mysteriously died."

"Some of the sheep at Wath Riding have died, too." I told him.

"Indeed!" he exclaimed. There was such an anxious look on his face I felt concerned.

"What's the matter, Reverend?"

"I'm afraid there's going to be trouble. The people of this moor are very superstitious."

"Trouble for who?"

"Jinny Thirkettle, I'm afraid. Poor woman. They think she's a witch. I find no amount of Christian teaching will change them."

He spoke in a depressed voice.

When we finished eating, the old man walked across to this desk, where I noticed a half-finished map lay.

"I'm still working on this one," he said.

I walked across and joined him. It was a map of the Wath area.

"To me, a map tells the story of the past. For example here . . . Where are my spectacles? Oh, here they are, I'm wearing them all the time. I get so absent-minded these days. One day I'll forget to give the Sunday sermon. That'll upset them, won't it?"

I could not resist a smile.

"Now, where was I? I remember—when the Romans came here, Yorkshire was part of the kingdom of the Brigantes, and these Brigante names are perpetrated in the names of the rivers, such as Aire and Wharfe. Now, in the ninth century Danish invaders arrived. Here you are, Denby—it simply means Dane's farm. Am I boring you, my child? I do tend to get carried away."

"Oh, no!" I exclaimed. I was glad to listen to him and forget my problems for a short time.

"Well, in the tenth and eleventh centuries Scandinavians arrived. We usually call them Vikings. Here is Janet's Foss. Foss is the Viking name for waterfall, and Janet was the local queen of the fairies. She is still reputed to work some kind of magic!"

His finger traced Wath Cliff, the lake, Wath Moor, and Hawksgill, then moved east along Grisedale. Toward the end of the dale I noticed a small circle.

"What does the circle stand for?" I asked.

"It means a circle of sacred stones. Laid down by ancient man, long before the dawn of our civilization."

I looked past the sacred stones to the end of Grisedale, which opened out into a small valley, on the far side of which was a range of fells marked "The Thrangs." On the other side of "The Thrangs" was a small dale marked, "Widdale," and on the banks of the river that flowed through it the parson had marked a cross.

"What does the cross stand for?" I asked curiously.

"As you know, this map is incomplete, but that cross stands for a ruined castle—Mallerstrang Castle. It was built by the Normans on the site of an earlier castle that belonged to King Arthur. The Normans built many castles up here in the north, mainly to help rule the rebellious natives, but I think this one was for hunting purposes.

"The Malloughby family owns it now, but they have no interest in the place. It's so far from Winterburn I doubt if Sir Matthew or his agent have visited it in the last twenty years."

"Sir Matthew owns a great deal," I commented.

"He owns us all."

Was there a touch of bitterness in his voice? A country parson without a private income was at the mercy of his landlord.

"I think I'll continue working a little longer on this map. Go to bed when you wish, my child. There's a candle on the mantel. Mary will be here in the morning. That is, if she can arouse herself after the festivities of tonight."

As I lit the candle I noticed a month-old copy of *The Leeds Intelligencer* lying on a chair, and a heading caught my attention: "Marquis of Rockingham Calls for Government Action to Stamp Out Coiners in the West Riding of Yorkshire."

"Anything troubling you?" asked the reverend from his desk.

"Oh, it's nothing, Reverend . . ."

"Your room is the first on the right at the top of the stairs. My sister uses it when she pays me her annual visit at Christmas. Good night, my child, and sleep well."

I climbed the stairs, and at the top entered the room the Reverend Butterwick had indicated. The floor was scrubbed and spotless, and against one wall was a handsome bed with an overhead canopy of black oak and dark red curtains draped from it on either side. As the parsonage was owned by Sir Matthew, I assumed this splendid bed had originally come from Winterburn Hall. Anyway, it looked very comfortable.

I undressed quickly and sank into the feather bed, staring at the flickering shadows the candle cast on the walls.

I thought of Leah, and wondered what the next day would bring. Perhaps if I asked at the cottages nearby, someone might remember her. I had to find her.

Then I thought of Seth, and the love that had suddenly sprung to life between us . . . a love that could never be. He would wait for me in vain. My pillow was wet with tears as I fell asleep.

When I awoke the next morning the sun was shining, and I could hear the plaintive sound of a curlew calling. It was somewhere over the fell that rose steeply from behind the parsonage. I went to the window and looked out, feeling a deep well of sleepy contentment within me. Then the harsh voice of Jack Reddihough, in the yard below, brought me sharply back to reality.

I dressed quickly. I would have to make an early start, and on reaching the ground floor passage a most appetizing smell of fried bacon and freshly baked oatbread was coming from the kitchen. A young woman in a crisp cap and apron, carrying a tray of crockery, opened the kitchen door.

She stared at me sullenly. This must be Mary Reddihough.

"You the young woman what stayed here last night?" Her tone was distinctly unfriendly. I felt like an intruder. Did she guard her parson jealously from all outsiders? Then I realized that a lone woman begging for shelter late at night must arouse feelings of distrust.

"I'm very grateful to the reverend for his kindness," I said, following her to the empty front parlor.

"Where you from?" she demanded, as she took the teapot off the tray and set it on the table.

"Calverley, near Leeds," I replied.

"My Jack hates Leeds!"

I wondered if that was where he had been branded.

Hearing a step in the passage outside, I turned to find Jack Reddihough himself standing in the doorway. The brand mark on his cheek puckered angrily at the flesh. At first he appeared not to notice me.

"Where's Reverend, Mary?"

161

"He's not up yet. I'll give him a call."

Then he looked at me.

"Mistress Nunroyd!"

The tone was mocking.

"What are you doing here?"

Then, catching sight of his wife lingering curiously at the door, he said, "I want to speak to Mistress Nunroyd privately."

As his wife sulkily closed the door he took a few steps toward me. I did not like the expression on his face. He made me think of a fox.

"Saw you last night with Seth. I know your game!"

"What do you mean by that?" I exclaimed indignantly.

"You're after the money."

"What money?"

"The forty guineas. Don't pretend you don't know. The brass what informers get like Harry the carrier were after. Know why he never lived to collect it?"

I shook my head. There was something about this man that frightened me.

He lowered his voice to a whisper.

"'Cos I hanged him."

Then he put his face uncomfortably close to mine.

"And I'll hang you too if you turn informer!"

I caught my breath, and I could feel my legs shaking. Little did he know I was an informer, but not for such a commonplace reason as gain. No, I had done it for a high-minded principle. I was being a good citizen.

"Good morning, Jack. Good morning, Mistress Nunroyd. I hope you slept well."

The Reverend Butterwick walked across the room, cheerful and smiling.

"Well, Jack, I'm glad to see you're making our visitor feel at home. Now I want you to get started on that roof. Such an annoying business. Whenever it rains I have to put a bucket in my bedroom to catch the rainwater. Ah, the trials and tribulations of being a poor country parson."

"I'll start straight away."

His manner was now dutiful and respectful, and as he left the room we sat down at the table, but my appetite had gone.

"Come, child, you're not eating. You may have a long way to go, and the food will give you strength."

He was right of course.

I watched Jack Reddihough climb the ladder outside the window and disappear onto the roof as I drank the scalding tea.

"Good fellow, Jack," observed the reverend. "Do anything for me. Very obliging. Very loyal."

"Did you finish the map last night, Reverend?" I asked politely, changing the subject.

"Oh dear me no. It takes many weeks to complete one. My parish duties come first. For example, this morning I must visit a sick woman at Denby Farm in Grisedale. In which direction will you be traveling this morning?"

"I don't know," I replied sadly.

"Have you no clue as to where your sister may have gone?"

"Only one, and I'm afraid I don't understand it."

"What is it?"

"Jinny Thirkettle said, 'Follow the ley.'"

"Ley—ley—I've never heard of it."

"Neither have I."

We ate in silence for a while.

"Probably a very old word. I must admit Jinny's a strange old woman. She never attends my church."

I looked away. I would keep Jinny's secret. She had enough troubles.

At that moment there was a knock at the front door, and I heard Mary Reddihough speaking to the caller. Then she opened the parlor door.

"Ned Pickering to see you, Reverend. He wants to know what it is you want doing."

The reverend rose to his feet.

"Excuse me, Mistress Nunroyd, but I must see Ned. I want him to cut the grass around the gravestones. It's quite a disgrace. I asked him to do it weeks ago and nothing happened."

The Reverend Butterwick left the room and I lingered a moment at the breakfast table, wondering if anyone in Hawksgill would remember Leah. Suddenly I remembered I had left my neckerchief in the bedroom, and on passing the kitchen door, I heard the sound of weeping. I hesitated a moment, wondering what to do. Then, giving a gentle tap, I entered.

Mary Reddihough sat at the table in a distressed state, her hands covering her face.

"Mary!" I exclaimed. "Whatever is the trouble?"

She paused in her weeping to answer me.

"I feel that sick," she said wiping her eyes. "I'd like to go to Jinny's and get something for it, but there's too much to do here. I've got to wash all them plates, and then get on with a broth. Reverend's very fond of broth."

I made a quick decision.

"You go to Jinny's straight away, and I'll wash these plates and prepare the broth."

She looked at me in amazement.

"I mean it," I said. "And I'll explain to the reverend when he returns where you have gone."

"You'd do that for me?" She looked astonished.

I took her cloak from behind the door and handed it to her.

"I'm sorry I was sharp with you this morning," she said apologetically as she fastened it. "But what with not feeling well—I'm like this every morning now, and Jack's not an easy man to live with."

I could believe that!

"I suppose I took it out on you. I'm sorry."

"Don't give it another thought. How long have you been married, Mary?" I asked her as she moved toward the door.

"Three months," she said, blushing. "I know what you're thinking, and you're probably right. But I must go to Jinny just to be sure. It's sort of comforting to go to her, and happen she'll have something that will make me feel better. I'll tell Jack what a good turn you done me today. Ta, ra."

And she was gone.

There must have been a week's dirty dishes in that bowl of hot, soapy water I thought, ruefully. Still, I said I would do it, and rolling up my sleeves I set to work. When I finished I turned my attention to the broth.

The vegetables were already piled up on the table, and I set to peeling, washing and slicing, then dropped them into the black cooking pot bubbling over the fire. Salt to taste, and a sprig or two of herbs, and the broth was done.

I returned to the front parlor. The reverend had still not returned, and having nothing to do I walked across and idly looked at his map. He had added Rosesett Abbey, which seemed to be a few miles east of Mallerstang Castle.

"Follow the ley—the track runs straight."

Jinny's words ran around and around in my head. It was useless. I could make no sense of it. The words were utterly meaningless to me. The more I thought of it the more frustrated I became.

Then suddenly I seemed to see a pattern in the map! I picked up the reverend's ruler that was lying nearby—I noticed he had carefully carved his name in the wood "James Josiah Butterwick"—and laid it on the map. The line from the reverend's church, past the sacred stones, to the ruined castle, finishing at Rosesett Abbey, was straight.

The track runs straight. Could this be the "ley" Jinny referred to?

It was a shot in the dark, but it was worth trying.

CHAPTER 14

There was a step in the passage outside, and the Reverend Butterwick entered the room.

"Well, let's see if Ned can get that grass cut. I do hate to see the graveyard neglected. He should have done it at Easter, but I'm afraid Ned isn't what one would call a fast worker. Still, he does his best and I must count my blessings. Now, Mistress Nunroyd, you're looking pleased about something."

"I think I've made a discovery. What do you think of this?"

The ruler was still in position on the map, and I showed him the straight line from the church to the abbey.

"Perhaps this is a 'ley.'" I said, looking at him hopefully. "It's a straight line, and Jinny said the track runs straight."

The Reverend Butterwick bent over the map, frowning thoughtfully.

"Could be just a coincidence, my child. I don't want to raise your hopes."

He studied the map for a few minutes before speaking again, but now I detected eagerness in his voice: "Did you notice that all these places are either sacred ground or of great antiquity?"

I hadn't, but was that a link?

"It's worth trying," I said.

"It is, but don't expect too much. Where's Mary?"

"She's feeling ill this morning," I replied. "And she wanted to see Jinny Thirkettle. So I hope you don't mind, Reverend, I told her to go while I did her chores. The dishes are washed and the broth's made."

"Are they, indeed," said the reverend, looking pleased. "That is good of you, Mistress Nunroyd. I'm sorry Mary's not feeling well. Hope it's not serious. Well, I suppose you'll be wanting to be on your way. I'll be able to accompany you down Grisedale, as far as Denby Farm. Before you go, take some bread and cheese from the kitchen for your lunch. You'll be hungry by the time you get to the end of that dale."

"Thank you, Reverend. You're very kind. I do appreciate it."

Hastening to the kitchen, I cut some bread and a piece of cheese. Then, taking the neckerchief from around my neck, I wrapped them up carefully into a small bundle.

We left the house soon after, setting off at a brisk pace across the village green, and took the lane, which was little more than a narrow cart track, down Grisedale.

It was a delightful day with a light breeze, so that the sun did not make walking uncomfortable. The reverend was a good companion, and kept up a stream of interesting topics as we went along.

"I find this growing apathy toward religion most worrying," he said. "There are some families who never come near the church, except at Christmas, and I've been thinking recently of introducing music into the service.

They do it in the big towns and cities, so why not at Hawksgill?"

"And why not!" I agreed enthusiastically.

"This farm I'm going to visit now. Mr. Bradley plays the cello, and his son, Tom, the fiddle. We could start off with those two, and add as we go along."

"I think it's a good idea," I said.

The lane was bordered on either side by a limestone wall. Where trees grew, the wall was encrusted with moss, thick as emerald velvet, and the grass verge in front of the wall was rich in purple foxgloves and frothy ferns.

Beyond the wall lay fertile fields of barley and oats, and meadows where lazy cattle grazed. The barley was well grown, and the summer breeze sent ripples through it like the waves of the sea.

"I believe you are feeling happy today, Mistress Nunroyd," remarked the reverend.

"I am," I answered, smiling at him.

"Happiness is a gift from God," the reverend replied. "If you are fortunate enough to receive it, cherish it, for it is the most precious possession you will ever have."

"I think you have this gift, Reverend," I remarked as we took a rest on a great stone that lay by the side of the lane. "And also you only see the best in people."

"It's the only way to live, my child," he replied. "I have lived a great many years, and alone, and in my solitude I have learned a little wisdom. Come, we must be on our way. Mistress Bradley will be thinking I've forgotten her."

As we proceeded, I noticed the dale started to narrow and twist. Around the next bend Denby Farm came into view; a prosperous looking place with the barn and house under one roof. The windows were freshly painted and sweet williams bloomed beneath the parlor window.

As we entered the farmyard, a young man carrying a rake appeared from the barn.

"Morning, Reverend. Morning, mistress. Mother will be right glad to see you. She's been asking for ye all morning."

"Sorry I'm a bit late, Tom. Got delayed. I see your barley's doing well."

"Aye, it is that. Let's hope this fine weather lasts; then we'll be harvesting a month from now."

"Now, Tom, you don't get many people coming down Grisedale. It's a bit off the beaten track. Would you remember a young woman passing here last November. It would help if you describe her, Mistress Nunroyd. This lady is looking for her sister."

I described Leah as best I could, but when I finished Tom Bradley shook his head.

"I don't remember anyone who looked like her. Mind you, it is a long time ago now."

I expected a disappointing reply, and it must have shown in my face.

"Don't take it to heart, my child." said the reverend gently. "You may still find her yet."

"I hope so," I replied sadly. "Thank you for all your kindnesses to me, and I hope I can repay you one day."

"Indeed, you do not have to repay me at all. All part of a parson's day. God go with you, my child, and I hope you find your sister."

He shook my hand warmly. I watched the two men enter the house, then I turned and continued on my way. I felt a little sad to leave the reverend, for he had had a soothing effect upon my troubled spirits.

Soon I could no longer see Denby Farm. Another bend

in the dale, and it was gone from view. Now the scenery was changing. There was no stone wall on either side of the lane. The fertile fields and meadowland gave way to rough moorland where sheep grazed, and a beck chattered over the stones close to the lane. Watercress grew there, and a pretty yellow flower called lady's bonnet, an exotic looking bloom, rather like an orchid. There were some growing close to the bank, and I leaned across and picked one. The one I picked had a solitary red spot on the lip—like a drop of blood! It was a bad omen to pick a lady's bonnet stained by a red spot. Just a foolish old wives' tale, but I threw the flower away.

The grass between the beck and the lane had been cropped short by the ever-hungry sheep. I took off my shoes and walked barefoot. It was like walking on velvet. I continued in this way for about half a mile, then suddenly I saw it—the circle of sacred stones.

I felt excited. Hoisting up my gown, I splashed across the shallow beck, my toes wallowing in the warm sandy bed. When I reached the opposite bank I started to run over the soft grass where the harebells bloomed, and up the slope.

There were several stones in all, each about five feet high and about ten feet apart, positioned in a large circle. Such strange shapes, like twisted, distorted human figures, waiting, watching. What had they watched in another civilization? Human sacrifice? Or was it something innocent like dancing on midsummer's eve or paying homage to the moon?

I sat down at the outer edge of the circle and ate my bread and cheese, thinking about the leys. Were they lines of power—some power ancient man possessed now lost in the mist of time. Were they means of navigation,

or their road to heaven? Jinny would know. I threw a piece of bread to a couple of green finches darting between the stones. Then, brushing the crumbs from my gown, I stood up. It was time to be on my way.

The dale was coming to an end, and just ahead of me the lane petered out into a bridle path which climbed into the next dale.

I put on my shoes and started walking.

When I reached the top of the pass I paused. Below me lay a small valley, and on the far side lay the highest fell I had ever seen. It rose from the floor of the valley like some gigantic whale. This must be the Thrangs, and Mallerstang Castle lay on the other side. Beyond that was Rosesett Abbey.

I wondered if I would have the strength to climb such a high, steep fell. It looked dangerous, too, and I could imagine myself slipping and falling to the valley below, with no one to hear my cries for help.

I was filled with doubt. Perhaps I was following the wrong ley. Jinny may have meant one running in the opposite direction from Hawksgill that had not been on the Reverend Butterwick's map. Or maybe this wasn't a ley at all. A ley could perhaps mean something entirely different, and not an alignment of sacred and ancient sites.

Then I felt angry. The truth was I was losing my courage, and looking for an excuse to give up and go back. Go back to where? I could not return to Wath Riding no matter how much I longed for Seth's arms to hold me. I had successfully pushed him from my mind all day, and now he came creeping back. He was my sister's husband, and I had no right to his love. I had no alternative but to go on. Whatever the outcome, good or bad, there was no turning back. I asked God to give me courage.

Clambering down into the little valley, sheep my only companions, I started to feel better. Then across a short area of moorland, and I was at the foot of the Thrangs.

I started the climb, following the narrow sheep track that twisted its way up the fell. Soon I had to pause for breath. There was a light wind, which I found cooling after the heat of Grisedale.

Up and up I went, my legs aching; the higher I went, the stonger the wind blew. Sometimes I had to push a sleepy sheep out of the way, and it ran off startled, bleating loudly.

After a while, the sheeptrack became a rocky staircase, and the intensity of the wind was such I had to keep a firm hold onto the rocky crags for fear of being blown over the edge.

I could scarcely believe it when I reached the top—a flat plateau of tough cotton grass with pools of dark, stagnant water. The wind tore at my gown and billowed it out like a cloud as I walked across the fell top to the other side, and gazed down into a wild, windswept dale.

No fertile fields here, no cattle grazing, but the heather was a purple mist and a river ran through it like a silver ribbon. On the banks of the river was Mallerstang Castle, just as the reverend had said. The agony of the climb had been worth it.

All that remained of the castle was the keep—a gaunt, square structure of stone, castellated at the roof. Adjoining it was part of a wall containing what had been the main gateway. The rest lay in piles of crumbled stones and masonry upon the ground.

I started the descent, but as the castle drew nearer, to

my dismay I could see no sign of life. Was it just a deserted castle lying in ruins, the home of owls and bats and any stray creature that needed shelter?

Then my heart quickened, for I thought I saw someone. I stopped and shaded my eyes and looked again, but there was no one there. Perhaps I had imagined it? I continued climbing down and when I reached the floor of the dale I could see details of the castle quite clearly. The windows were small, arched medieval ones, with one larger than the rest. The door of the keep was set in a richly carved Norman arch.

I hurried anxiously across the heather, scrambled over the piles of stones that had once formed the towers and walls, and onto a cobbled area before the keep.

Suddenly, to my amazement, I could hear the sound of children's voices. Then three small boys ran out of the keep—clean, though their clothes were ragged—and commenced to kick an old ball over the cobbles. No one took the slightest notice of me. They looked healthy and well cared for. Then a small, bare-footed girl appeared and stared shyly at me. She, too, was clean; her long fair hair had been carefully combed, but her little gown was so badly torn it scarcely served its purpose.

I walked up and smiled encouragingly at her.

"What's your name?"

"Nancy."

Then she disappeared inside the open door of the keep.

How strange—a ruined castle full of children! Feeling perplexed, I wandered round the outside of the keep. What would Sir Matthew think?

The river was about a hundred yards away, and not a soul in sight. I started walking toward it, and as the sound of the boys' shouting grew fainter I became conscious of

another sound.

It was a woman singing!

It was a melancholy song, the notes carrying on the still, evening air. I knew that voice! Ahead of me was a small gulley, and I started running.

I reached the top of the bank and looked down. A young woman with her back toward me was standing on the bank of the little beck. She had long brown hair, and was wearing a green gown. Suddenly she turned.

It was Leah!

CHAPTER 15

I shall never forget the haunting sadness in her eyes. It is something that will remain with me always. I rushed down the bank and flung my arms around her.

"Leah! Leah! At last I've found you. I thought I would never see you again!"

"Dear Damaris. My beloved sister!"

We were weeping together, both overcome at our reunion. When our emotions subsided a little, Leah wiped her eyes.

"How did you find me?" she asked.

"It was Jinny."

I thought Leah looked frightened.

"Jinny? No one knows I am here. Oh, Damaris, so much has happened."

"Let's sit down on the bank and talk," I suggested.

As Leah moved to sit, I noticed her body was thick and heavy.

She was with child!

She caught my startled look and turned away.

"Do not judge me like the world and punish me. I have been punished enough."

"Oh Leah! I would never punish you. And what is so wrong in expecting Seth's child?"

"It's not his child. Please do not look so shocked. I did not marry him."

"You did not marry him?" I repeated, astonished. Her words did not make sense. "But when you eloped with him we all assumed . . ."

"I know. But it's a long story . . ."

"Please tell me, Leah. I want to know everything."

She leaned her head against my shoulder.

"It seems so long ago now, that morning when we reached Wath village. I remember we stopped for breakfast at the inn before going to the church, and I remember thinking I had never felt so happy. Then Seth said, 'We'll soon be wed and your dowry will buy back the Paslew land.' Then everything changed. It was the first time he had mentioned my dowry, and I told him there was no dowry. Instantly he was angry, and in that moment I knew father had been right. Seth was only marrying me for the money. He asked me why I had waited until then to tell him, and I told him I didn't think the money was important. And he replied: 'Not important, what kind of world do you live in?'

"I think I grew up that day. Oh, Damaris, I was so distressed! Then Seth went on: 'I know your father hated me and that is why we had to run away, but I assumed that once we were wed, everything would be alright.'

"It was terrible to learn the truth. Whether Seth still wished to marry me now that there was no dowry, I did not care, but I told him I would not marry him."

"What did you do then?"

"I was in a dilemma, for my pride would not let me return home; I had brought disgrace on them and I could not let them suffer more. We decided to go to Seth's father's farm until I decided what I must do.

"That first week at Wath Riding was a living nightmare. I did not know what to do. I felt confused and frightened. Bella was a kindly soul, but she didn't know what to make of it. The old man treated me with contempt, and as for Seth, I think the situation just caused him embarrassment. My feelings had changed toward him and I could not bear him to come near me. At night I slept in the cupboard bed.

"At the end of the week Seth proposed to me again, but this time I was sure it was out of pity. I refused him. I thought of him as a grasping, mercenary man, who had shown no consideration for my feelings. I had been such a fool. Those evenings we had walked along the banks of the Aire, he had never told me he loved me. I had assumed he did. I was so naive about men. He was the first man who had courted me, and it had gone to my head.

"Seth told me that if I wouldn't marry him, I must return home. But I couldn't, Damaris. I told him I had decided to become a governess. It seemed the only way out of the terrible situation I was in.

"I wrote a letter to a newspaper placing an advertisement, and gave it to the carrier in the village. On my return I was surprised to see a visitor had arrived for Seth. It was Widd Malloughby. He said he was staying at Winterburn Hall, and on hearing that Seth was back and good at repairing guns, had brought a pistol with him for Seth to examine. I thought him very pleasant, and the next day they went out shooting together. After that Widd came to the farm frequently, and seemed to prefer Seth's company to that of the gentry.

"It was a bitter life for me. I had expected so much—now there was nothing. It was about that time that I came to realize that Seth was involved in something clandestine. On the days Widd did not come, I would hear Seth leave the house after dark, and then I would not hear him return until dawn. I never asked questions because we rarely spoke.

"One day a revenue man called and searched the house. I met him later in the village and questioned him about it. He told me he was looking for evidence of coining. I naturally could tell him nothing, but from then onward I was suspicious of Seth. The meals improved and he started wearing expensive clothes.

"Widd called one day when Seth was out and questioned me about his activities. I told him nothing, for after all I owed Seth a certain amount of loyalty. He gave me a roof over my head.

"I was now feeling a little concerned, for it was taking so long to receive replies to my advertisement. I remember deciding to take a long walk across the moor to Hawksgill. I thought it would revive my stale spirits. I had no sooner set off when I met Widd. He was on horseback, and asked me if I would like to go with him into Settle. Having nothing better to do, I agreed.

"He told me he was curious about my position at Wath Riding. I told him everything, and from that day a bond of friendship was forged between us. I began to look forward to his visits to Wath Riding, for now he made life worth living for me. For the first time in my life I had found a man whose happy, carefree manner put me completely at my ease, and I found I could talk to him in a way I could not talk to other men. Seth had always frightened me a little—his personality overwhelmed me.

"One day I received a reply to my advertisement. It was from a lady in York who had one small girl, and wished me to commence my duties after Christmas. I replied, accepting her offer.

"Widd came to the farm that afternoon and I told him my news. To my surprise he begged me not to take the post but to marry him instead. I was astonished. I had not realized that our friendship had blossomed into something deeper for him. I felt unsure of my feelings and I refused him. I was also afraid of being hurt again.

"Damaris, you must be tired and hungery, and I cannot stop talking. Let's go back to the castle. Mistress Priestley will be returning soon."

"Priestley! I had heard that name before. Could she be the missing sister-in-law of Lady Priestley? We climbed out of the gulley and started walking slowly toward the castle, its ancient stones mellowed in the fading light.

"Widd left the farm that afternoon, depressed," continued Leah. "And after that his visits ceased. I told Seth I had accepted a post with a lady in York, and would like to stay at Wath Riding until after Christmas when my future employer wished me to take up my duties. He reluctantly agreed.

"I missed Widd's company so much I began to wonder if I had done the right thing by refusing his offer of marriage. At the beginning of November I heard from Bella that he was to marry Clarissa Priestley. Bella was friendly with the housekeeper at Winterburn Hall and had received the news from her. I was devastated, for the knowledge I had lost him forever made me want him desperately. The anguish I suffered—the sleepless nights when I tossed and turned in that little bed. I felt my life was not worth living.

"A few days later I was alone in the house. Bella had gone to Jinny to get something for the old man. Snow had come early and the wind had blown it up into deep drifts on the moor. Seth and his father were out rescuing the sheep. It was a wild night, with the wind blowing the snow against the windows. I sat by the fire thinking about Widd, and how foolish I had been because I had not had the courage to accept his love when he offered it. Then my thoughts turned to Seth, and a conversation I had had with him when he urged me to return home and not become a governess. Suddenly I heard knocking at the front door; to my amazement, Widd was standing there. I had thought I would never see him again. He told me he had come to say goodbye because he was leaving for America very soon.

"I think I started crying, and then he took me in his arms."

Leah covered her face with her hands.

"And he seduced you, Leah?"

She nodded. "It was like trying to hold back the tide. I struggled with him, but I wanted him so much I had little strength to resist him."

"He made love to you and now you're expecting his child?"

"Yes," she whispered. "Widd was leaving just as the men returned. He told Seth his horse had cast a shoe and would have to leave her behind. He proposed taking the short cut across Wath Cliff. The old man volunteered to show him the way, and I decided to go too. I had to know about Clarissa, for he had said no word about her or our future together during the entire evening.

"The snow was deep, but the wind had died down, and it had stopped snowing. As we climbed the slope, I remember having the strangest feeling that I would never see Widd again. When we reached the lake I was afraid I would not get a chance to speak to Widd alone, so, noticing the old man was getting tired, I told him to return to the house, and I would show Widd the way.

"Widd and I continued alone. I remember we walked in silence with Widd carrying the lantern, and all the time I was thinking I must ask him now if he intends to marry me, but I could not find the courage to say it.

"Then suddenly we were on the cliff top. I remember thinking it was dangerous to stand so close to the edge, but at that moment I am ashamed to say I was more concerned about Widd's intentions, and I said, 'Widd, after what has happened between us tonight, do you intend marrying me? You asked me once before and I refused you.'

"I can see his face now in the lantern light, smiling at me.

"'Of course I will. Why do you think I came to the house tonight?'

"'And what about Clarissa Priestley?'

"'Don't take notice of servants' gossip!'

"Then it all happened so quickly. He moved as if to take me in his arms, but his foot must have slipped on an icy patch. He stumbled a moment, tried to regain his balance, then fell with his legs dangling over the edge, his hands clawing at the icy snow.

"I grabbed one of his hands and tried to hold him, but it was no use. I could feel him slipping from me, and then he was gone!

"I stood alone on the cliff top like someone paralyzed. It was as if I could not grasp what had happened. One minute Widd had been standing at my side, smiling and happy, and the next he was lying dead at the foot of the cliff. I remember I tried to scream, but no sound came."

"What happened after that?"

"I ran all the way back to the farm and told Seth what had happened."

We reached the walls of the castle, and approaching us along the bridle path was a woman dressed in black, riding a black horse, against an evening sky of pearl gray.

"That's Mercy Priestley," said Leah enthusiastically, waving to her. "She's been a guardian angel. If she hadn't found me on the fells, I would be dead now."

The woman rode up to us and dismounted. She was in her middle years. Her gray hair was drawn away from a devout face, and in her severe black gown she looked like a nun. She smiled kindly at me.

"Mercy, this is my sister, Damaris. She came looking for me."

"I'm glad you found her," she replied as she dismounted. "Leah wouldn't let me write to her family, you know. Which way did you come? I didn't notice anyone on the way."

"I came by way of the Thrangs."

"Then you must indeed be weary. Our fare is simple, but you are welcome to join us."

I thanked her. As she led the way through the gateway in the broken wall and across the cobbled courtyard, she told me what a great help Leah had been to her.

"There have been times when I don't know what I would have done without her," Mercy said.

The three boys were still playing football.

"Where do the children come from?" I asked curiously.

"They were abandoned in the streets of our cities,"

replied Mercy. "One of the most disgraceful things of our modern society. We have cities filled with poverty and human misery that is beyond the imagination. Every time I go into Leeds or Bradford I always bring an abandoned child back. My greatest need at the present time is clothing."

We passed through the arched doorway and entered a large, lofty hall with a vaulted ceiling. Stone ribs ran up to a heraldic rose at the crown of the vault. This was all that remained of the castle's former grandeur. There was a huge hearth in one wall where a girl, older than the rest, was stirring something in an old cooking pot. In the center of the hall ran a roughly hewn trestle table with benches on each side. About half a dozen ragged urchins, all of a tender age, were racing about. The din was deafening, but as Mercy entered the room, as if by magic, the noise ceased.

"Now children, you are not attending to your duties. Polly, set out the bowls, and you'll need to lay one extra tonight. We have a guest. Jimmy, fetch the spoons, and Sammy, we need more water from the river. You know where we keep the bucket."

Leah went to the trestle table and commenced cutting slices of bread and supervising the preparation of the meal. I could tell by the way the children spoke to her that they were very fond of Leah. When the meal was ready, Mercy took her place at the head of the table, and the children stood at their places on either side. Mercy joined her hands together and bowed her head; the rest of us, did likewise.

"For the food we are about to eat, dear Lord, we thank You, and may we love and serve You all the days of our life."

Then there was a scramble to sit down, with the benches scraping on the stone floor. It was a simple meal of porridge, slices of haverbread spread with honey, and drinking water from the river. The children looked healthy, but Mercy certainly was in need of clothing for them. Everyone wore ragged clothes and was barefooted. I counted five boys and seven girls. It was obvious they were happy in their new life. The little boy on my left told me enthusiastically how sometimes he caught fish in the river and the would eat it for supper, and the little girl opposite told me proudly that Mistress Mercy had taught her to bake cakes on the griddle. I could not help noticing how well behaved they were, and wondered how Mercy achieved it. I asked her afterward as she watched the children clear the table.

"I never beat them. My only punishment for wrong doing is to deprive them of their supper, and everyone hates being sent hungry to bed. Every child has his or her duty, and no one shirks it, for they know it is the only way we will survive. My only worry is Sir Matthew Malloughby. He owns this castle. I know him very well, and I knew he would never allow me to turn it into an orphanage. I was so desperate I just moved in. I know the law will say I am in the wrong, and it worries me at times. But what can I do? My resources are limited, and I could not afford to rent a house in Settle. One day he will come here and throw us out."

"I met you sister-in-law, Lady Priestley, and her daughter, Clarissa, the other day," I commented.

"How are they—the same as usual?"

I nodded.

Leah was now busy taking the children to bed. I watched her escorting them up the spiraling flight of steps, the children clutching the stone handrail carved into the wall. I followed them.

The first floor led into a large chamber with mattresses of straw upon the stone floor.

"This is the boys' dormitory," she said. "We need blankets before the winter comes. We are double the number we once were. Now, boys, don't forget to say your prayers. Sleep well."

We continued to a similar chamber on the next floor. "This is the girls' dormitory," explained Leah. "Mercy sleeps with the girls, and I sleep downstairs in main hall. I'll get a mattress so that you can sleep near me."

Leah bid the little girls good night and we returned to the hall. The fire was still burning, and I noticed a cradle in the corner.

"We were lucky to get it," Leah said. "Mercy brought it from a little farm a few miles from here."

We sat down before the fire and Leah gave the smouldering embers a stir with an old poker.

"The evening following Widd's death," she continued, "I was sitting alone in the front parlor trying to decide what to do. I had to get away from Wath Riding at all costs, for now it was unbearable.

"Seth came in and we started quarreling. I told him I believed he was a coiner and it should stop. He was very angry and went out soon after—I think it was to the lake cottage.

"I spent the rest of that evening sewing. I remember deciding it was time for bed, when the old man came in. I didn't like the way he looked at me. It made my blood run cold. I knew he had never liked me, for he considered that I was the cause of Seth's downfall, but that night there was something evil about him.

"'I followed you last night,' he said, looking at me with a strange expression on his face.

"'So you saw Widd fall over the cliff?' I asked.

"'No,' he said, shaking his head. 'He didn't fall, you pushed him over.'

"'You must be insane to say such a wicked thing!' I cried.

"'I've watched you ever since you come to live here,' he said. 'You decided Seth weren't good enough for you, and after that you set your cap at squire's nephew. But that weren't easy. I reckon you were just a plaything to him, and when you heard he were marrying Lord Priestley's daughter, you got desperate, what with him going back to America and all. So you came with us last night, and told me to go back to the house. When you were alone on cliff top, I reckon he told you he'd finished with you, so you pushed him over. You murdered him, and I'll tell Sir Matthew and you'll hang for it! Murderer! Murderer!'

"He was screaming at me.

"I was never so terrified in my life! I ran from the room, out of the house, and onto the moor."

Leah was shivering at my side. I put my arm around her.

"I know what happened from then onward," I said.

"Damaris," she said, laying her head on my shoulder, "I'm afraid of tomorrow."

CHAPTER 16

"Don't be afraid, Leah. You have me to help you now. And don't worry about the old man. Bella thinks he's weak in the head, and after what you have told me, I believe it. Anyway, the verdict was suicide."

"Suicide? It was an accident."

"There was the evidence of Widd's depression."

"That was after I turned down his proposal."

"I have visited Sir Matthew, and rest assured, no one has been to him with such a dreadful accusation. And there was no mention of any betrothal between Widd and Clarissa Priestley. It was just servants' gossip."

"Oh, Damaris, if I hadn't been so worried about Clarissa, and not gone to the cliff with him, perhaps he would still be alive today."

"Don't dwell on such thoughts," I said. "Keep to the facts."

"You're so wise, Damaris."

I did not feel very wise at that moment.

Leah gave a yawn. "I shall sleep well tonight," she said, as she settled herself down on the mattress. In a few moments I could hear her gentle breathing.

I lay down on the mattress next to her, staring into the deep well of darkness above me. It was difficult to sleep, my mind teeming with a thousand things. It was obvious the old man had wanted to frighten Leah away. There was no doubt that he hated her, but was he also afraid she would discover Seth's coining activities, and inform on him? No wonder he had not made me welcome.

If Seth had not persuaded Leah to elope with him, none of this would have happened. And all for the greed of her dowry. I fell asleep with angry thoughts about Seth.

When dawn pierced the keep with shafts of pale, quivering light, I awoke with a sensation of unhappiness. Leah was still in a deep sleep by my side—sleeping like a child.

It was obvious she could not stay at Mallerstang Castle indefinitely. Mercy could barely feed the children she already had. She would have to stay here until I decided what should be done, then I would come back for her.

Leah, mother of a bastard child, its father dead before he could wed her. I knew the punishment for such a misdemeanor. A rich woman got away scot free, but a poor woman did not. She had to walk barefooted through the jeering crowds, wrapped in a sheet, to the church to do penance. Why was the man never punished? The injustice of it filled me with despair. Whatever happened, I vowed my sister would never suffer such humiliation. She had been punished enough.

It was Friday, the day Sir Matthew had asked me to return and sign the statement. If I did not go, he might go to Wath Riding, find Seth's cellar and arrest him. I had to protect Seth—whatever wrong he had done. I could not be the cause of his downfall. How I rued the day I had gone to Winterburn Hall, so impatient to tell my tale. When Seth knew what I had done, how he would despise me. But what could I tell Sir Matthew? I could not sign the statement because it would endanger my life? Or I had told lies for revenge?

I was eager to be gone.

"Leah," I whispered, "I must go, but I shall return."

She did not stir. I bent down and kissed her on the cheek.

As I crossed the hall Mercy came down the steps, and we walked together into the courtyard outside.

"Leaving so soon?" she asked.

"I must. And will you tell Leah I shall be back. I have many things to do, but all will be well. Tell her to trust me."

"I'm sure she will," Mercy answered. "Which way are you going?"

"I want to go to Wath village."

"You can avoid climbing the Thrangs. Go up the dale and after about four miles, you'll see a small farm on the left. You can't miss it—it's the only farm for miles. A young woman lives there, and Fridays she takes her cart into Hawksgill and Wath to sell her produce. If you hurry you'll catch her."

I thanked her for her great kindness to Leah, and for giving me shelter for the night. Then I set off, following the bridle path that ran alongside the river. I turned back once and waved. Mercy was still standing at the castle gateway, a somber figure in her black gown; behind her the dawn sky was pale green, and the clouds were the color of apricots.

Soon the rough moorland ground gave way to fertile fields where oats and cabbages grew, and ahead lay the farm Mercy had told me about.

It was a modest place. The same style as Denby farm with the house and barn under one roof. A horse and cart stood in the farmyard, the cart loaded with cabbages. I had been lucky. Then a young woman came out of the house, climbed up onto the cart, and with a flick of the reins the cart drew slowly out of the yard.

She was young. I should say in her early twenties—buxom, with yellow hair straggling untidily from beneath her cap, and a round friendly face that broke into a grin when she saw me.

"Want a lift?"

"Please."

"Jump up then."

I climbed into the seat next to her, and we set off at a good trot over the dried up, dusty cart track.

"My name's Jill. Jill Hardy."

"I'm Damaris Nunroyd."

"Where you making for?"

"The Wath area," I replied vaguely.

"You have a lot of cabbages." I remarked.

"Yes. And I won't be back until I've sold every one. Probably be dark when I get back."

"Are you not afraid of being out alone at night?"

"Why should I be afraid?" she asked, surprised at my question.

"You may be accosted by a stranger."

"Never my luck, especially handsome ones."

She laughed, then her expression became solemn.

"Seriously, there's such a shortage of fellers 'round here; you wouldn't believe it. I mean, I'd like to get wed and settle down, but what chance have I? Mother and father are dead. Father died three year last candlemas, and mother followed him next year. It were as if she couldn't bear it without him. So you see, I run the farm on my own. It's only a small place, but it's hard doing everything yourself from sunup to sunset. Besides, it gets lonely.

"Of course, there's Ned Claughton. I like Ned, but he's that slow. I'll tell you what I mean. We're coming home from a dance, and the moon's shining, and everything romantic like. He puts his arm 'round me, and I says 'Yes, Ned?' and he says, 'Daisy's not giving milk.' I get that exasperated with him!"

"Well, Jill, if you think Ned will make a good husband and you'd be happy with him, you'll have to do the proposing."

"You're right there."

She was thoughtful for a moment.

"You come from Mallerstang Castle?"

"Yes, I have."

"I hear it's full of ragged children. The woman who runs it, Mistress Priestley, she comes down to buy stuff of me sometimes. I let her have an old cradle the other day. Well, takes all sorts, don't it?"

I agreed it did.

Widdale was a long, twisting dale which verved in a south westerly direction, so that after about five miles we were traveling roughly parallel with Grisedale. Jill never asked about my private business, for which I was truly grateful, and she kept up a cheerful thread of happy chatter as we went along.

Suddenly, over to the right, I saw a spectacular waterfall in a cleft in the fellside. As we drew level Jill stopped her cart, and for a few minutes we watched the water cascading down over the rocks.

"That's Janet's Foss," shouted Jill over the roar of the water. "If you throw a penny in and make a wish, it will come true."

I shook my head. "My wishes don't come true."

We continued on our way and soon entered Hawksgill.

"Where is everyone?" asked Jill, looking around. The village was deserted. She brought the cart to a halt by the village green. There was not a soul in sight save for an old man sunning himself at a cottage door.

"Where is everyone?" called Jill, but the old man did not answer.

"Serves me right. I'm forgetting he's as deaf as a post."

I wondered where the Reverend Butterwick was: working on his map, visiting his parishioners, or writing his Sunday sermon. At that moment I did not wish to meet him. He would ask questions, and how could I truthfully answer them and not bring shame on my sister.

"Well, best be on our way," said Jill, giving the reins a shake. "Next stop Wath, and let's hope I can sell my cabbages there. I'm too late for Settle market now."

We set off up the steep road that crossed Wath Moor.

"My father always called this place coiners' moor," said Jill, lowering her voice.

I made no comment, and we passed Thwaites farm. Here again there was no sign of life. The road leveled out and, as Jinny's cottage came into view, I saw with astonishment that it was surrounded by an angry mob.

Jill gave her horse a touch of the whip and the old cart rattled quickly over the bumpy road. Whatever it was, it was bad.

We drew up at the fringe of the crowd. There were about twenty men and women. Some of the women had brought their children, and most of the men were armed with sticks and rakes. They stood in Jinny's garden, crushing her precious herbs and flowers.

Then I heard a man shout, "Come on, we're wasting time. Bash that door down!"

A young boy was standing apart from the rest, silent, as if ashamed to join in. I jumped down from the cart and spoke to him.

"What has Jinny done?"

"They say she's bewitched the sheep," he answered.

The faces in the crowd were hard with hatred as they chanted in unison: "Hang the witch! Hang the witch!"

And there was Mary Reddihough shouting with the rest. Mary, who only yesterday had been so eager to go to Jinny for help. And Mistress Thwaites—she too went whenever her children were sick. All of them in that crowd had gone to Jinny at some time to cure their illnesses, or for advice when they were in trouble. Now they had turned on her. Their treachery sickened me. Then I saw them for what they were—frightened people looking for a scapegoat.

The news had obviously spread that there were dead sheep at Wath Riding and Thwaites Farm. They had put the blame on Jinny, and they were going to kill her for it. The mood of the crowd was frightening. Someone threw a stone through the window, shattering the glass, and I suddenly thought of poor Jinny, cowering and trembling behind her door with only her cat for comfort. Suddenly the crowd no longer frightened me, and I pushed my way through. I got to the front and stood with my back to Jinny's door. I didn't care what they did to me.

"The sheep are not bewitched!" I shouted with all my strength. "They are diseased."

197

"You talk like a city woman," said a big brutish fellow, reeking of brandy. "Keep your nose out of matters that don't concern you."

Then it all happened so quickly. He pushed me into the crowd as if I were a sack of potatoes. I fell to the ground, dazed and bruised. The crowd surged forward, people fell on me, and soon I could not breathe. As I was losing consciousness, I heard a voice louder than the rest, and the crowd fell back, silent.

I first saw his boots. I knew those boots, and I knew that voice. I looked up, and Seth was towering over me, his face drained of all color. He was brandishing a horse whip.

"Get to your homes, or I'll horse whip the lot of you," he shouted. "There'll be no more hangings on this moor."

The crowd moved away, muttering, deprived of their victim. Seth held out his hand and helped me to my feet.

"They'll not try to harm that old woman again," he said grimly.

"Seth . . . if—if you hadn't come . . ." I stammered, brushing the dirt from my gown and hair. Then I looked into his face, and there was that deep, hurt look in his eyes.

"Why didn't you come?" he said. His voice was very low.

"There was something I had to do. I've found Leah. She's expecting Widd's child."

"Widd's child? And where are you going now?"

I could not tell him, and I could not bear to look at him any longer. I walked across to Jill and climbed up next to her.

"Let's get to Wath village as quickly as we can."

We set off at a brisk trot. I could feel tears pricking behind my eyes. I did not dare look back.

"You were brave, Damaris! Standing up to that crowd. I couldn't have done it," Jill remarked as we passed Wath Riding. I wondered what Bella was doing, and the old man, and if my burned out candle had been discovered in the cellar.

"That man with the horse whip. Wasn't that Seth Paslew? Now he's what I call a man. See the way he handled that crowd. It'll be a lucky woman who gets him. Are you feeling alright? You're as white as a sheet."

I had to admit I did not feel well.

"Here," she said, reaching into a pocket in her voluminous skirt. "I always keep a drop of something on me. You never know when you might need it."

She brought out a small flask and unstopped it.

"Take a swig of that."

I took a swig. It was brandy, and its warmth flowed through my veins, reviving me, giving me courage.

The ordeal of meeting Sir Matthew lay ahead, and every mile brought me closer. And what of Christian? He would call me a turncoat.

We were now entering Wath village.

Jill pulled the cart to a halt by the Woolpack.

"I'll be leaving you now, Jill," I said. "I'm very grateful to you, and I hope you sell your cabbages."

"Well, I'm not going back until I have."

I jumped off the cart.

"Here, you never told me where you come from?"

"Wath Riding."

"Isn't that where that Seth Paslew lives?"

I nodded. "Goodbye, Jill, and thanks."

I left her looking after me with a puzzled expression on

her round, friendly face.

The signpost to Winterburn was just beyond the village. I set off along the winding lane, a desperate sort of feeling inside me. The sun was hot and I wished I had my straw hat to give me protection. I had to save Seth, undo the damage I had done. The fact that he was committing a crime and should be punished did not occur to me. I could only think emotionally, and at the same time, my feelings toward him were confused. I could not deny he had treated my sister badly.

Soon I was walking up the drive of Winterburn Hall, and the house came into view. I must see Christian first—the matter of Widd's child was not for Sir Matthew's ears.

I was wondering where I would find Christian when I saw a man come out of the stables and begin feeding the peacocks that strutted proudly to and fro in the stable courtyard.

"Could you tell me where Master Christian is?"

"He's in the stables," he said, looking at me curiously.

I entered the first door. There was a long line of loose boxes with a flagged passageway to the left. The mingled smell of leather and hay filled my nostrils. Here Sir Matthew kept his hunters and carriage horses. Beautiful, sleek animals, worth a fortune. The light was dim, and at first I did not see Christian. Then, hearing a clattering at the far end, I looked up and saw him. He was with the little bay filly that Sir Matthew had bought at the horse-fair.

"Damaris," he called, and I hurried up to the filly's box and leaned over.

"I've been so worried about you," said Christian, leaning on the barrier and looking intently into my face.

"If you hadn't come today I would have gone up to Wath Riding to find out what was happening. I also want to see the old man."

"I've found Leah!"

He opened the door of the loose box and stepped out. "Where is she?"

"Mallerstang Castle. And I know about Widd's death. It was an accident."

We went and sat on bundles of hay in the corner.

"How do you know?"

I told him everything, and when I finished he sat a long time, his chin resting in his hands, a faraway look in his eyes.

"What shall we do, Christian? Leah won't go home."

"Where is this Mallerstang Castle?"

I gave him instructions suggesting the route Jill and I had just taken. A groomsman entered the stable at that moment.

"Saddle my horse, Rob. I'm leaving straight away."

"Righto, sir."

"What are you going to do?"

"I don't know," he replied as Rob led his horse into the yard. "All I know is I must go there."

He mounted his horse.

"I presume you want to see uncle about the statement. He's expecting you. You'll find him in his studio." There was a clatter of hooves over cobblestones and he was gone. Then I stood alone. The ordeal was at hand. I turned and entered the side door.

There was no one in the passage, and I entered the deserted great hall. Christian had said Sir Matthew was expecting me, so I climbed the stairs. Strangely, there were no servants about. At the top of the stairs the studio

202

door was open. I stepped inside and looked around, but there was no sign of Sir Matthew. The large canvas of Wath Cliff was still on the easel. It dominated the room.

It appeared finished, and I walked up to it curiously. Sir Matthew had added the figure of a woman who was lying spread-eagled at the foot of the cliff. Her face was turned toward the viewer. Horrified, I realized it was me!

I was lying dead at the foot of Wath Cliff! If was macabre! Why should Sir Matthew wish me dead? I knew too much? Too much about coining? Dear God, what was I entangled in—was this the headquarters of a nation-wide coining gang with Sir Matthew at the head? How did Seth get all those coins? It was a well-run organization, and Seth could not possibly do it alone. The day I took the bag of coins to Settle and bought the bills, was probably on Sir Matthew's instructions. What a cunning way of getting rid of clipped coins. And the other men, the men who came to the meeting the night they hanged poor Harry, did Seth give them money he was too busy to handle himself?

I must get out of this house. I could smell the danger like a cornered animal. Somewhere in the house a door closed, and my nerves tautened like a violin string.

I ran from the room and down the stairs. The great hall was empty. Now the silence was charged and ominous. I went to the door through which I had just entered, the door that would lead me to the stableyard.

It was locked!

I tried again. How strange! It had been open just a few minutes ago. I could feel my heart quickening as I hurried across the hall to the great front door. This too was locked!

Walking slowly to the center of the room, I could feel

tension building up in me, twisting my stomach, my hands wet with sweat. It was more than a coincidence that both doors were locked. Far away, I could hear the distant mutter of thunder.

There was one remaining door, and that led into the library. I turned the knob, and to my surprise it opened. There seated at his writing cabinet facing me was Sir Matthew. He was watching me like a cat watches a mouse.

"Come in, my dear. I've been expecting you."

I stood in the entrance, breathing quickly, my body tense, the fear of death blotting out all sensible thought.

"Where's Christian? Have you seen him?" Sir Matthew asked.

"He's gone to Mallerstang Castle," I managed to say, my throat dry as dust. And as soon as I said it I realized my mistake. I should have pretended Christian was still here.

"You've come to sign the statement about Seth Paslew. It's very good of you."

Suddenly I noticed there was a solitary glass of red wine on his cabinet. I had a strange feeling it was intended for me. Sir Matthew rose to his feet, pulled the bell sash, and, picking up the glass, walked toward me.

"This wine has been waiting for you, my dear. I thought it would refresh you after your long walk."

He held out the glass for me to take.

"Drink it, Damaris."

I did not move. If I drank that wine I was as good as dead. He stepped closer and held the glass of rich crimson liquid close to my face. In the distance I heard the chiming of the village clock.

"Drink it!"

There was a sharpness in his voice I had not heard

before. I looked into his eyes. They were like dead eyes, cold, without feeling, and all I could hear was the ticking of the clock on the occasional table.

Then I heard the door close behind me, and footsteps crossed the room. I saw Sir Matthew give a swift nod, and as I turned I caught a brief glimpse of Beckwith before a pair of hands tightened around my throat.

CHAPTER 17

I awoke to find myself in what appeared to be an outhouse used for storage. It must have been a stable at one time, for the smell of horses and hay still lingered. The room was filled with an accumulation of unwanted items, such as empty sacks, broken harnesses, and wheels. A pair of cart shafts leaned against one wall, and nearby were a few sacks of grain. The walls were covered with dirt and cobwebs. In the far wall was an opening covered with rusty iron bars, and to the left of it a ladder was fitted to the wall leading to the loft.

A rat scurried across the floor and disappeared into one of the sacks. I sat up, feeling dizzy. My throat was sore, and my neck felt hot and uncomfortable. Overhead the rain was hitting the roof with frightening ferocity. I stood up, and walked across the room to the opening. Through the iron bars I could see a wood growing close to the outhouse. I had to get out of here! I shook the bars but they were firmly embedded in the wall.

I next turned my attention to the door. It had a latch type of opening, and to my surprise the latch had been removed. All I had to do was lift the bar that the latch would have lifted, and I was free. It seemed too easy. With trembling fingers I lifted the bar, and the door swung open. Of course, this was the way we secured outhouses at home. There was no need to bother with locks, for once the latch had been removed the door could only be opened by reinserting it.

About twenty yards in front of me was a long stone building, which I guessed to be the rear of the stable block. There was no one in sight. With beating heart I ran into the wood, the trees engulfing me with protective arms, concealing me, their clean, fresh smell filling my nostrils. On and on I went, half blinded by the pelting rain, never daring to look back, not sure where I was going, except away from that hideous place, and thanking God my life had been spared. I gasped for breath, stumbling over half-hidden tree roots, but I dared not stop. Then I caught an impression of movement from behind a tree, a horse whinnied, and suddenly someone's arms enfolded me fiercely.

It was Seth! Thank God it was Seth! I buried my face into his cloak, panting for breath. I felt I wanted to cry, but no tears came.

"They tried to kill me!" I panted. "They left me for dead . . . Beckwith and Sir Matthew. Beckwith tried to strangle me!"

He did not speak, and I could feel his hand running through my wet hair.

"Why are you here, Seth?"

"I found your burned out candle in the cellar." There was disillusionment in his voice. "Then I asked Bella if she knew where you had gone, and she told me of her suspicions. I'll say this for Bella, she's loyal."

"Seth, let me explain . . ."

"You can do that some other time," he said bitterly.

I looked up at him. His eyes were cold and dispassionate. I've lost him, I thought desperately.

"Never trust a woman!" he said sourly.

"Don't talk like that," I pleaded.

Then he grasped my hair, tilting my head back, and a gruff sort of embarrassment crept into his voice.

"But I'm a fool, like all the rest."

And he kissed me in a desperate sort of way that made me want to cry.

"I was so worried about you," he whispered, "that I came here to find out what was happening. Sir Matthew said you had called earlier to say goodbye. He said you were on your way home and Christian had taken you to Settle in the carriage. I had a feeling something was wrong. I was certain you would not have left me so abruptly. I went to the coach house. The carriage was still there, and one of the grooms said Master Christian had taken his horse and gone off alone.

"I was very suspicious, and decided to hide in these trees to see what happened next. If you look across here you'll see we have a good view of the drive."

I looked in the direction Seth pointed, and as I did, I heard the sound of galloping hooves coming down the drive. Beckwith rode past, his cloak billowing out behind him like a black cloud.

"Riding as though the devil himself was chasing him," whispered Seth. "I'm going to the house to see what's happened. It looks as though the rat's leaving the sinking ship."

"I'm going with you, Seth."

Roxanna had been tethered to a nearby tree. Seth untied her and we mounted. Then, carefully picking our way through the trees, bending low to avoid overhanging branches, we came out onto the drive and proceeded toward the house.

It was twilight, and when the house came into view in that strange half-light one gets before darkness, it was easy for the imagination to go astray. As I sat behind Seth on Roxanna I could not control a shiver, for to me it was now a house of terror.

Seth touched my hand reassuringly as we entered the courtyard. We took Roxanna into the stables, then entered the house through the side door.

I never thought I would have the courage to enter that house again, but Seth's presence gave me strength. An elderly woman appeared in the passage, somberly dressed in a dark gown and white cap and apron. I judged from the keys that jangled at her waist that she was the housekeeper. She appeared very agitated.

"Mr. Paslew, the master's dead!" she cried. "I've just found him in the library. Come this way."

We hurried after her into the great hall and through to the library, the scene of my attempted murder. There, in the gray light of dusk, the body of Sir Matthew lay sprawled upon the carpet.

A scared servant rushed in with a candle and handed it to the housekeeper, and in the light of the candle we saw "The Luck of Winterburn" smashed into half a dozen fragments upon the carpet. He had tole me, "When it breaks, our luck breaks with it." I bent down and picked up the pieces.

The housekeeper gave a cry, and sank weeping into a chair. Seth knelt down and looked closely at Sir Matthew.

"You'd better send Rob for a physician. He's still breathing."

Sir Matthew was carried reverently up the great staircase by two manservants, while Seth, the housekeeper and I stood watching below.

"Doctor Chadwick lives at Settle," said the housekeeper, wiping her eyes. "I can only pray he's not out visiting when Rob gets there."

"I'll sit with Sir Matthew until the doctor arrives," Seth said.

"That's very good of you, Mr. Paslew. Where's Beckwith? I can't find him anywhere."

"I don't think you'll be seeing Beckwith again," said Seth as he walked toward the staircase. "He's gone."

"Would you like to wait with me in my room?" asked the housekeeper, turning to me. "It's very odd about Beckwith."

I thanked her and followed her down a passage at the rear of the house where she showed me into a comfortably furnished room. She placed a small kettle on the fire.

"We'll have a cup of tea while we're waiting," she said, sitting down and indicating a chair for me.

"I believe I've seen you here before, Mistress . . ."

"Nunroyd. Yes, I have been here before."

"I remember now. I caught a glimpse of you the day you came back with Sir Matthew from the horsefair. Poor Sir Matthew—it must have been the shock of breaking the luck. His heart wasn't very strong. I know he used to boast how fit he was, but I knew the truth. I'm Mistress Hardaker, by the way."

The kettle was now boiling and Mistress Hardaker brewed the tea. How I longed to speak to Seth alone . . . to clear up the misunderstanding that had arisen between us. But there was no chance now. If I had lost him, it was my own fault, I thought bitterly.

Mistress Hardaker poured the tea into two china cups.

"I always keep these for special occasions," she said proudly, handing me one.

It was the best tea I had ever tasted and I told her so, but Mistress Hardaker was not interested. Her thoughts were of her master.

"He won't last, I know it," she said sadly, her eyes filling with tears. "And it'll never be the same again. I've served him all my life, and my mother before me."

Mistress Hardaker sipped her tea slowly.

"Master Christian's late," she observed, looking up at the clock. "He's never as late as this as a rule."

There was a bowl of red roses on the table—the first of the season, deep dark crimson, the petals just unfurling from their tight buds. Father grew such roses at Calverley—the dark ones were his favorites. There was always such a bowl in the house in the summer, filling the room with their heady perfume. When Leah and I were children, the smell of roses was always in the house. We were happy then. The world had not touched us. I wanted it to be like that now, I thought, with no sorrow or fear.

"I've had some happy times here," continued Mistress Hardaker. "When Sir Matthew were younger, he used to give masked balls. All the gentry for miles around came. What nights they were—the champagne flowed like water, and there was dancing till dawn. After that he became very fond of Italy. Spent a great deal of his time there. That's where he learned to paint."

I had a sudden vision of that painting upstairs. The horror of it was as strong as ever. One day I would ask Christian to destroy it.

"Of course I know nothing about painting," Mistress Hardaker added, "but I have heard he's quite an accomplished artist. Anyway, in the last few years he had to cut down on his spending. No more trips to Italy, half the housemaids we used to have, and entertainment's on a very small scale compared to what it used to be."

"Why did he have to cut down?" I asked curiously.

"Living beyond his income—mortgaged up to here. It was his gambling that did it. As he got older, it got worse—it was like a fever with him."

This was a side to Sir Matthew that was totally unknown to me, and I wondered if he had won Wath Riding in a gambling game. Just then there was a knock at the door.

"Come in," called Mistress Hardaker.

It was Rob. "Doctor Chadwick's with him now."

"Thank you, Rob. And tell doctor I'd like to see him before he goes."

He nodded solemnly and closed the door.

"Rob's very reliable. More than I can say for some around here. How's Bella? I used to see a lot of her at one time."

"She's very well," I replied, my thoughts far away.

I looked up at the window. It framed a black sky hung with stars, and I wondered if Christian had found Mallerstang Castle. A loud hammering on the door startled me, and in walked a portly gentleman with a large red face, followed by Seth.

"Doctor Chadwick!" exclaimed Mistress Hardaker, rising to her feet a little flustered. "What is the news?"

Doctor Chadwick shook his head mournfully.

"I arrived too late. He's dead. His heart, you know. Well, he was a very old gentleman, and this could have

212

happened any time. I'm very sorry."

The color fled from Mistress Hardaker's face and she sat down.

"I was expecting it," she said, her eyes filling with tears.

"We'll all miss him. He was a good man."

Mistress Hardaker echoed his words, wiping her eyes on her apron.

"His lawyer will have to be informed," continued Doctor Chadwick. "I'm seeing Mr. Bingley tonight. I'll tell him if you like; it will save Christian the trouble."

As the doctor left the room I looked at Seth.

"Did he say anything?" I asked.

"He never regained consciousness," Seth replied.

We bid goodnight to Mistress Hardaker and I thanked her for her hospitality. She accompanied us down the passage into the great hall where, to my astonishment, Christian and Leah were entering at the front door. She was leaning on Christian's arm, fragile and vulnerable as a flower in a cold spring. I rushed forward and embraced her.

"Leah! What a wonderful surprise. I had no idea Christian was bringing you back!"

Seth smiled at her, and in his smile was compassion. She returned his smile, but there was such weariness in it I felt afraid.

Looking at Mistress Hardaker, Christian said, "Give Mistress Leah a comfortable room. Good night, Leah. If you want anything, just ring. I'll see you tomorrow."

As Leah left the hall with Mistress Hardaker, Christian continued: "Miss Priestley lent me her horse, and she's riding over tomorrow on Rebel. I'm going to persuade uncle to put her orphanage on a proper business footing."

"I'm sorry, Christian," I said as gently as I could, "but we have bad news for you. Your uncle has just died. He had a heart attack. He's upstairs."

"Excuse me, I must go up immediately."

Looking tense, Christian hurried up the stairs, and I went and sat in the window seat and looked at the figurine of the Greek nymph. I had to control myself. I could not weep here. In a few minutes Christian came hurrying down the stairs.

"How did it happen? He was alright when I left."

"He broke 'The Luck of Winterburn.' It must have been that."

He sat down in the window seat next to me.

"Poor uncle. He believed that legend. Well, they all did here."

Then Christian suddenly looked sharply at Seth, who was standing in the center of the room.

"What brings you here, Mr. Paslew, at this time of night? And Damaris, what is the matter with your neck?"

"Beckwith tried to strangle her," said Seth, walking up to us.

Christian looked startled.

"Beckwith! I don't understand. Sit down, Mr. Paslew."

Christian pulled the bell sash.

"Now what's this nonsense about Beckwith?"

"It was on your uncle's instructions. I was left for dead in an outbuilding," I told him.

Christian searched my face as if begging me to say it was not true.

"I'd rather not talk about it," I said.

"I'm afraid we'll have to," he replied. "Why should he try to do such a terrible thing?"

"I knew too much."

"I'm sorry but I don't follow this. The last time I saw you, you were on your way to sign a statement you had made about Mr. Paslew. You discovered he is a coiner. Is that not correct?"

"It is," answered Seth. "I am a coiner."

I could not look at his face.

"I still don't follow why my uncle wanted Damaris dead."

"You won't like it," said Seth grimly.

"Go on, I want to hear it."

"I worked for your uncle."

"What do you mean 'worked'?" asked Christian, puzzled.

"I clipped and coined for him. He was the leader of a coining organization. Damaris had become too dangerous to remain alive. She discovered what was happening at Wath Riding, and it was only a matter of time before she discovered what was happening here."

Christian looked thunderstruck.

"I can't believe it. My uncle. Squire, magistrate, a respected citizen. It doesn't make sense."

"Well, it's true."

There was a long pause. Then Christian spoke in an irritated tone.

"Where's Beckwith?"

"Beckwith isn't here," said Seth.

"Where is he?"

"I have no idea, but I don't think you'll be seeing him again. We saw him galloping out of the gates as if all the devils in hell were on his tail."

"I could do with a brandy," said Christian.

He pulled the bell sash again, but no one came.

"The servants appear to be disorganized tonight," said

Seth. "I know where the wine cellar is. I'll get it." And he walked off in the direction of the door which led to the side passage.

Christian and I sat a moment in silence. It was an embarrassed silence, then he turned and looked at the garden in the midnight darkness.

"You've changed, Damaris. Something's happened. The way you look at that coiner. You almost look as though you've fallen in love with the man."

I did not answer.

"He's a common criminal and he'll hang for it. And I thought you were so sensible and level-headed."

"I cannot help myself, Christian." I could not keep the bitterness from my voice. "You have no need to worry on my account. What man will love a woman who has been as treacherous to him as I have been to Seth."

"Treacherous? You were doing your duty."

I heard Seth's footsteps crossing the great hall. He was carrying a bottle of brandy and three glasses.

To my relief he seemed relaxed; the tension had gone from his face.

"I knew I'd find it. I've been coming to this house since I was a boy."

He poured the brandy into the glasses.

Will you take brandy with us, Damaris?" Christian asked.

I nodded. It would dull the pain I suffered every time I looked at Seth.

"You were telling me my uncle was leader of a coining gang. I want to know more details." I thought Christian's tone was sharp.

"Beckwith brought the money," said Seth, sipping at his brandy. I could see that Seth was relieved to tell his story. "He always came to the lake cottage after dark. He never went near the farmhouse, said he might be seen. He wanted us to meet in some isolated spot, so the cottage seemed just the right place. Well, he would hand the money over, and I would deal with it. Then, whenever it was ready, he would collect the clipped coins and the newly minted money. Sometimes I was instructed to buy I.O.U.s with the clipped money. But Sir Matthew never had any difficulties with the newly minted coins, because the dies had been stolen from the Mint."

"Anyone else involved?"

"There were the other men on Wath Moor. They took what I couldn't handle. Sometimes the quantities involved were quite large."

"Where did my uncle get the money from?"

"He had his own money, and then of course he had his contacts—the corrupt gentry, for a start."

"I presume my uncle did it because he was in financial difficulties," said Christian, looking worried. "I know he's had to economize in recent years."

"He was a desperate man," said Seth. "His debts were piling up and it was the only thing he could think of—apart from selling his land, and that he would never do. You see, this area has always had a reputation for coining, but always on a small scale: a weaver clipping the odd guinea when he could lay his hands on one. In the past, Sir Matthew turned a blind eye to it."

"You should never have agreed to coin for my uncle," Christian said, annoyed.

Seth banged his fist on the table.

"I had to. He blackmailed me!"

There was an expression of incredulity on Christian's face. He refilled Seth's glass.

"Tell me about it."

"One day shortly after I returned with Leah, I had occasion to come here to pay off a bit of rent father owed. Father owed about six months—he was hopeless with money. While I was in the agent's office, Sir Matthew came in and remarked about the money we owed, and I begged for time. Then he said he wanted to talk to me in his library. He gave me a glass of champagne to celebrate my homecoming, so he said, but I knew there was something in the wind. Sir Matthew didn't hand out champagne to tenants for nothing, especially those owing rent. Then he said, 'You're just the man I'm looking for, used to working with metals. I'd like you to help me win a wager.'

"I've always known Sir Matthew was a gambling man. He'd take a wager on anything—cards, horses, any crazy venture. It was an obsession with him. I said, 'What is it this time?' He gave me a queer sort of smile and said, 'Dicky Fox said he could tell a counterfeit coin at first glance, and I said he couldn't. So I've wagered him fifty guineas. Well, will you help me win my bet? I have the dies and moulds, everything you should need. He made me look a fool last year over those fake paintings, and I swore I'd get even with him.' He was like a schoolboy.

"I said, 'You're asking me to risk my neck so that you can win a bet. No thank you, Sir Matthew.'

"'So you're worrying about the law,' he said. 'You're forgetting, I'm the magistrate. So you can stop worrying about that.'

"'I can't do it,' I told him. 'It's wrong.'

"'Come, come,' he said, 'look who's talking, the man who owes me six months' rent. Do you not consider it wrong to owe me money?'

218

"I told him I'd get a job and pay him back.

"'You won't,' he said. 'There's a slump in the iron trade right now. You won't find it easy to get another job.'

"He was right. I was in a difficult position.

"'For goodness sake,' he said, 'I'm only asking you to help me win a bet. Tell you what—if I win it, I'll cancel the rent you owe me. Now that's fair, don't you agree. If you don't, I'll give you twenty-four hours to get out. What's the matter with you, Paslew? I'm just asking you to make a few coins for a bit of fun.'

"He owned Wathdale, and everyone in it," said Seth sourly. "He pulled the strings and we danced."

"So you made the coins?" asked Christian.

"Yes, I did," answered Seth, draining the glass. "The worst day's work I've ever done in my life. Anyway, at the time I thought that was the end of the matter. Then about a week later Sir Matthew sent for me. Again, I was showed into the library, and again more champagne. I thought, if it's another wager, the answer is no, and he can evict us if he wants. I didn't care. Well, Sir Matthew was in a very good mood, and told me he had won his wager with Dicky Fox, and as I expected he asked me to make some more. I refused. I said he could evict us if he liked, but I wasn't doing it.

"Then he got nasty and said he could have me before the bench for coining and I would be hanged. And I said, 'But you told me to do it. You had a wager with Dicky Fox.' And he said, 'You're lying. I never said anything of the sort.'

"Then I knew I was beaten. He told me not to look so downhearted and he would see I gained from it. He said, 'I know what you Paslews want—you want your land

219

back. The land your grandfather sold to me. If you coin for me, you can have it back.'

"He tempted me and I fell."

"So you started coining on a regular basis?" asked Christian.

"That's right," replied Seth. "And a few days ago he called me up here and said, 'Just to show you I'm a man of my word, you can start off with the meadow in front of Wath Cliff.' But he hadn't given me anything. There was something growing there poisonous to sheep and I had to put them back on the moor."

"And have you received nothing from this . . . er . . . business transaction?" asked Christian.

"Except odd shirts and waistcoats he'd finished with. I took the crumbs from a rich man's table."

I could feel the rage boiling up in Seth.

"And of course he told me to keep Widd's horse."

"Widd knew about the coining, but he had no idea my uncle was involved," said Christian. "You've been treated very shabbily, Mr. Paslew. I had no idea my uncle was such a hypocrite. Were large amounts of money involved?"

"I've been clipping a hundred coins a day, plus what I've handed over around the moor. Then there was the tragedy of poor Harry. Harry went to Sir Matthew and informed on Thwaites. Sir Matthew had Thwaites arrested to avert suspicion. He was only on the fringe. Then Sir Matthew gave instructions for Harry to be hanged. I was sickened with the sordid business and would have nothing to do with it. Of course, when Damaris informed on me it was a different matter."

Seth paused. I could feel his eyes on me, and I wanted the earth to swallow me up. I wanted to run out into the darkness and never stop running.

"I was the principal coiner," Seth continued. "If I was arrested the whole organization would have collapsed.

"I urged her to find out anything she could," said Christian.

He was trying to help me. But it didn't ease the pain.

"Are you going to arrest me now?" asked Seth.

CHAPTER 18

"I will have to consult a lawyer on this matter," said Christian, looking very grave. "Will you come back tomorrow afternoon, Mr. Paslew, and I'll be in a position then to discuss the matter with you."

It was very late. We said our goodbyes, and I asked Christian to tell Leah we would see her tomorrow.

The night was dark, for the moon was in its last quarter, a silver crescent in the black heavens. Neither of us spoke. Riding pillion behind him, I leaned my head against Seth's back, wishing that so many things had never happened. My heart full of regret.

When we reached Wath Riding, the house was in darkness. We stood together in the passage before the stairs door. Seth looked drained of all his strength.

"Seth . . ." I began.

He put his hand up.

"Not now," he said wearily. "When you say your prayers, you'd better pray for me."

He turned and walked into the front parlor. I went upstairs and knelt down at my bedside and tried to pray. But my mind was numb. I climbed dispiritedly into the little bed. I've lost him, I've lost him, I said again and again to myself, and when I was weary of my thoughts, I tried to sleep. But sleep would not come. I was conscious of Seth downstairs, alone with his anguish.

Suddenly I could bear it no longer. I got up and crept down the stairs, and along the passage to the front parlor. He sat in the window seat, his face gray in the pale moonlight. With a choking cry I ran and knelt at his feet.

"Forgive me, Seth! Forgive me!"

I felt his hand touch my head.

"This above all, to thine own self be true," he murmured softly.

"This is the truth, Seth. I swear it. When I first decided to inform on you, I thought I was doing the right thing. At that time I was only concerned with being a good citizen, of doing my duty. Then when I met you at the lake something happened to me. I realize now it was love—I was falling in love with you. All I can tell you is that when I got to the village that day I was in an agony of indecision, something was holding me back. Then I met Christian, and I do believe if I had not met him I would never have gone to Winterburn Hall.

"Then at Hawksgill Feast I realized what had happened to me, that I loved you. The feeling I have for you only comes once in a lifetime.

"I went to Winterburn Hall today to try to save you— to retract everything I had said. I am so ashamed of my weakness, and how you must think of me with contempt."

I laid my head upon his knees and wept.

"I do not think of you with contempt," he said in a soft voice.

"If you die, part of me will die with you," I whispered.

He put his hand beneath my chin, and I looked up at him. His dark eyes were filled with tears.

"I am not worthy of such a love."

Then he drew me to my feet and kissed me, gently at first, then, as his passion became aroused, with such an intensity and hunger my whole body trembled.

Then he pulled away from me.

"Don't waste your love on me," he said huskily.

"Why?" I cried, my eyes blinked with tears, the ache in my heart so bad I wanted to die.

"I have a confession to make." His voice was hoarse and hesitant. "I am guilty of a despicable act. I eloped with your sister for her dowry. I was just a common fortune hunter."

"Seth . . ."

"Please let me explain. I was a desperate man—caught in the poverty trap. No matter how hard I worked at your father's forge, I would never have enough money to buy back the Paslew land. Do you know what it is like to have this burning desire to own your own land, and never to have the chance of acquiring it?

"When I met Leah, I saw my opportunity. Such a girl would have a very good dowry, I thought, and she seemed to like me. But, of course, I had not reckoned with your father, or Leah's impractical attitude toward life. I hate myself now for the misery I caused her. I have no doubt I shall be punished for all my wrong doings.

"When she refused me a second time, my pride was hurt, but she could have stayed here as long as she wished; I was never unkind to her. When she ran away I assumed she had returned home."

"She ran away because of your father. He accused her of murdering Widd Malloughby. Did he never tell you?"

224

I asked.

"Murdering Widd? How ridiculous. Didn't she know my father is as mad as a March hare. He's been like it ever since mother died. Leah should have come to me for advice. The night Christian questioned me about Widd, I saw no point in implicating her."

We sat talking until the first delicate light of dawn lifted the gloom of the parlor. Then I went upstairs, and, to my surprise, I slept. When I awoke it was late, for the sun was high over the barn. I dressed reluctantly, not caring, for the future was a dismal thing. I knew Christian was a merciful man, but at the edge of my mind there was a nagging fear, like a dark cloud.

As I came down the stairs, I witnessed an extraordinary sight: Bella, waving a broom was chasing Joe Shaw down the path that led to the moorland road.

I went into the kitchen, thinking of Seth. Only a strong man admits his weakness, I thought, as I put the kettle on the fire. Then I thought of the day at the lake when he had first looked at me with tenderness. Whatever happened today I would have that memory, and the memory of Hawksgill Feast. The memory of last night hurt, and I did not want to think of it.

As I brewed the tea the back door opened, and in walked Bella, her eyes blazing.

"That's last we've seen of him," she said, setting the broom down in the corner.

"Whatever's happened?"

"I found out why he come courting," she said, sitting down at the table, her face flushed from her exertions. "He come again this morning. Very pleasant, most agreeable, and I'm thinking, he still wants me, after all these years. Well, I made him a cup of tea, and I gave him one of my maids of honor—I'd just done a batch, and he said, 'These are good, you always were a good cook, Bella.'

"Then he starts asking questions again about Master Seth, and he come out with it straight: 'Is he a coiner,' and I said, 'I'm not saying he is, and I'm not saying he ain't.' 'Oh,' he says, 'when he bought them bills, why were *every* coin clipped in that bag he sent?' I said, 'You ask him. What you asking me for?' And he said, 'Don't you know, cos when I get the reward money, we can get wed.'

"I were that mad I picked up a broom and hit him with it, and I said, 'I wouldn't have you if you were last man on earth.' Then I chased him out of house. I reckon he won't stop running till he gets to village."

"Oh, Bella," I said, giving her a hug. "You did the right thing. You always know what to do."

I poured her a cup of tea, and handed it to her.

"Wherever have you been these last couple of nights? I've been that worried and so has Master Seth." She gave me a very sharp look.

"I've found Leah!"

"Where was she?"

"Mallerstang Castle. A Mistress Priestley has turned it into an orphanage and Leah was helping her. Christian Malloughby has brought her back."

"Where is she now?"

"At Winterburn Hall. She's expecting Widd Malloughby's child."

"I half expected it. That night when I come back from Jinny's, I knew they were upstairs. I couldn't tell you. I didn't want to bring shame on her."

"Don't worry about it. Where's the old man today?"

"Haven't seen him since last night. I'm worried and

I've told Master Seth. He's out looking for him now. Oh, I expect he's drunk somewhere. He always looks ill but there's nowt wrong with him, 'cept he drinks too much. Well, I'd better get on with my work. I thought of Yorkshire pudding today."

She rolled up her sleeves and poured out the flour.

"Only a Yorkshire woman can make Yorkshire pudding!" she said, laughing.

I looked through the window, and to my amazement, Seth was staggering across the yard carrying someone on his back.

It looked like the old man!

"Bella, look!"

I rushed to the door and flung it open, and Seth came in bowed almost double beneath the weight of the old man, water running from both their clothes.

I knew the old man was dead as we followed Seth through to the front parlor. Seth laid the old man on the floor, and the water from his clothes ran in little rivulets across the stone floor. His face was a horrible color, and his eyes had such a wild, agonized look in them, I had to turn away.

"You found him in the lake?"

"Yes."

Seth sat down, breathing heavily. "I remembered he talked yesterday about going fishing. When I got there I saw the upturned boat; he was floating nearby. He must have been up there when that thunderstorm broke last night."

"Perhaps he lost an oar, and as he reached for it the boat overturned," I suggested.

"And he couldn't swim," reminded Bella. "Poor man," she commiserated, wiping her eyes with her apron.

"Oh, Seth, I'm so deeply sorry," I said, sitting down next to him.

"Father and I have traveled a long, hard road." There was a distant look in his eyes as he spoke. "But he's at peace now. He was looking forward to the day when he'd join mother."

"You'll have to see Chris Lightfoot," said Bella. "And we'll give him a good send off. There won't be a sober man or woman on moor when we've finished burying him."

"We have an appointment at Winterburn Hall," Seth reminded me, rising to his feet. "We'll call at Chris' place on the way. He's a good chap. He'll see to everything. I'd better get changed, then we must go."

"Aren't you going to have a bite to eat?" asked Bella as we walked into the passage.

"We'll have it when we get back," called Seth as he hurried up the stairs. "Oh, Damaris, could you get me a tankard of ale? I need something to get rid of the taste of that lake water."

I walked through the kitchen and into the storeroom, thinking of his words: "When we get back." Another man would have broken under the strain, but not Seth.

I filled a tankard from the cask that lay on the table, and as I turned to go I noticed a small leather bag wedged between the cask and the wall. It was bright red with green drawstrings. Where had I seen such a bag before?

It was as we trotted along the moorland road on our way to Winterburn Hall that I remembered where I had seen such a bag. It was at Jinny's, and she had said they contained poisonous herbs—foxglove seeds for curing dropsy. No one at Wath Riding suffered from dropsy. I wondered if the old man had bought the seeds from Jinny

228

on the pretext he was ill, for the purpose of poisoning Bella. Seth had admitted his father was mentally disturbed. What was the motive? Was he afraid Bella would inform on Seth? How little he knew Bella. And the cat? Had he poisoned the cat? The cat had led me to the cellar; did he know that? Now I would never know the truth.

When we reached the village I waited by the packhorse bridge with Roxanna while Seth went across to Chris Lightfoot's cottage to make arrangements for the funeral. Suddenly my attention was drawn to the revenue man, the man who had searched Wath Riding earlier in the week. He was nailing a notice to the wall of the Woolpack Inn. I could not contain my curiosity, and walked across the road to read it, leading Roxanna by the reins.

It read as follows:

WHEREAS THE PRACTICE OF CLIPPING THE GOLD COIN OF THIS KINGDOM HATH FOR A CONSIDERABLE TIME BEEN CARRIED ON IN DIVERS PLACES WITHIN THE WEST RIDING OF YORKSHIRE IT IS THEREFORE THOUGHT PROPER TO GIVE THIS PUBLIC
N O T I C E
THAT BY AN ACT OF PARLIAMENT ANY PERSON GUILTY OF COINING, CLIPPING, OR DIMINISHING THE CURRENT COIN OF THIS REALM WHO SHALL AFTERWARDS DIS-COVER TWO OR MORE PERSONS WHO HAVE COMMITTED EITHER OF THE SAID CRIMES, AND GIVE INFORMATION THEREOF TO ANY ONE OF HIS MAJESTY'S JUSTICES OF THE PEACE IS THEREBY ENTITLED TO HIS MAJ-

ESTY'S PARDON FOR ALL HIS SAID
CRIMES WHICH HE MAY HAVE COMMITTED
BEFORE SUCH DISCOVERY, AND IS MORE-
OVER BY THE SAID ACT ENTITLED TO THE
REWARD OF FORTY POUNDS FOR
EVERY PERSON CONVICTED.

> WM. CHAMBERLAYNE
> SOLICITOR TO HIS
> MAJESTY'S MINT.

I felt so excited I could hardly contain myself. The innkeeper came out, scratching his head.

"Giving 'em a pardon," he said, "I don't understand it. Last week it were hanging. I tell you, government's in a panic."

"I disagree," said the revenue man. "They're sharp fellers in London, and they know the coiners are too clever to be caught red handed. Look at the hard time I've had."

He looked at me with his hard, gray face, and my heart missed a beat. Did he remember me?

"They know what they're doing," he continued. "Give 'em a pardon, and they'll all be out in the open. It's like putting a hound in a den of foxes."

I saw Seth coming out of Chris Lightfoot's cottage, and hurried across to him.

"Seth!" I cried, as soon as I reached him. "The revenue man has just put up a new proclamation. A pardon to any coiner who informs on two others!"

"What good is that to me? I'm not turning informer," he said in a harsh voice. I turned away from his stare. He'll never forget, I thought bitterly.

The main door of Winterburn Hall was opened by a

young footman who showed us into a study on the first floor. Christian was seated at a desk looking over a pile of documents. He stood up as we entered. How different he looked from last night. There was a warmth in his eyes that had not been there before. How different from Seth, whose eyes were full of pain. Christian indicated two high-back chairs with velvet seats.

"Please sit down, Damaris and Mr. Paslew. A very nice day. Not too hot. Just as I like it."

He picked up a flagon of wine.

"I've just discovered your heather mead. Delicious drink. I'm afraid we have nothing like this in Virginia."

He poured out three glasses.

"Leah gave birth to a fine boy this morning," he announced proudly. "He's premature, but strong. Just like Widd."

"A boy?" I exclaimed delightedly. "May we see her?"

"We'll go up in a moment," he answered, smiling, "She's sleeping right now. In the meantime, let's drink to Leah and young Widd."

We raised our glasses and drank.

"The family lawyer came this morning and told me I have inherited the Malloughby estate. It wasn't a surprise; uncle had already told me the contents of his will."

We murmured our congratulations.

"Now, let's get down to the serious business," he continued. "You have probably seen the new proclamation in the village. I instructed it to be displayed this morning. Under this new law, I am happy to tell you, Mr. Paslew, you will receive a pardon. I consider you have already informed on two coiners by telling me about my uncle and Beckwith—in my eyes they are as guilty as the

231

men who actually clipped and coined."

Seth pardoned! And he did not have to inform on any of the moorland men! It was a dream come true. Seth looked stunned. He was speechless.

"My uncle promised you the Paslew land. I am happy to return it to you. At least you'll be able to say the Malloughbys kept their word. Mr. Bingley will be drawing up the necessary deed of ownership for you."

"Oh Seth, how wonderful! It's what you've always wanted."

"That's very kind of you, Mr. Malloughby," was all Seth could say.

"One last point on this tragic business of Widd," said Christian, rising from his desk.

"Why was my uncle so contented with the verdict of suicide? He must have known that Widd was suspicious and making inquiries. Also, Widd was frequently at Wath Riding."

"Perhaps he felt the verdict of suicide was convenient," suggested Seth. "It could equally have been accidental death, but the servants came forward and gave evidence of depression."

"That was because Leah wouldn't marry him," I interjected.

"So, as far as he was concerned," Seth continued, "it was a satisfactory verdict because it cleared any of the coiners from suspicion."

"I think you're right," said Christian. "Come, let us go to Leah now."

We followed him along the corridor to a bright room looking south. There were white rugs on the floor and the great fourposter was covered in blue silk. Leah lay back on the pillows, a small bundle of humanity nestling in her arms. Her face was as white as the sheet, but there was a glow of happiness in her eyes that caught at my heart.

I kissed her warmly and touched the baby's tiny hand.

"He's beautiful, Leah," I said, with a lump in my throat.

"He's just like Widd," she whispered. "The same nose, the same mouth."

"I'm going to adopt him," said Christian, proudly, "And take him back to America. Of course, Leah won't be parted from him, so she'll be coming too."

"You've been so good to us," said Leah.

"I'm responsible for Widd's son," he said, touching her hand.

There was a look of soft tenderness in Christian's eyes as he looked at Leah.

Leah was going to be alright.

"Congratulations, Leah," said Seth, walking up to the bed. "You have a fine son. I once did you a great wrong. Will you forgive me?"

"Of course I forgive you, Seth." And he kissed her on the cheek.

We left soon after that, and as we rode along the lane the silence between us became oppressive. Once Seth turned in the saddle and I saw the anguish on his face. When we reached the crossroads just before Wath village, Seth halted Roxanna. To the right it said "Settle," and to the left "Wath Moor."

"I suppose you'll be going to Settle now to catch the stagecoach," he said in a hard, flat voice.

I dismounted and looked up at him, and the anger that had been building up in me exploded.

"What's the matter with you, Seth Paslew? Have you lost your courage? Am I not the woman you love?"

233

My tears blurred my vision.

"How can you love me after what I've done—fortune hunting, coining."

"What about me—I informed on you. How can I expect your love?"

Then he leaned forward and kissed me with such warmth and love that all the anger within me melted.

"Will you marry me, Damaris?"

"With all my heart."

After we left the village the road wound uphill all the way.

Somewhere overhead a lark was singing.

ENTRANCING ROMANCES BY SYLVIE F. SOMMERFIELD

TAMARA'S ECSTASY   (998, $3.50)
Tamara knew it was foolish to give her heart to a sailor; he'd promise her the stars, but be gone with the tide. But she was a victim of her own desire. Lost in a sea of passion, she ached for his magic touch—and would do anything for it!

DEANNA'S DESIRE   (906, $3.50)
Amidst the storm of the American Revolution, Matt and Deanna meet—and fall in love. In the name of freedom, they discover war's intrigues and horrors. Bound by passion, they risk everything to keep their love alive!

TAZIA'S TORMENT   (882, $2.95)
When tempestuous Fantasio de Montega danced, men were hypnotized. And this was part of her secret revenge—until cruel fate tricked her into loving the man she'd vowed to kill!

RAPTURE'S ANGEL   (750, $2.75)
When Angelique boarded the *Wayfarer*, she felt like a frightened child. Then Devon—with his gentle voice and captivating touch—reminded her that she was a woman, with a heart that longed to be won!

Available wherever paperbacks are sold, or order direct from the Publisher. Send cover price plus 50¢ per copy for mailing and handling to Zebra Books, 475 Park Avenue South, New York, N.Y. 10016. DO NOT SEND CASH.

FASCINATING, PAGE-TURNING BLOCKBUSTERS!

BLAZING CIVIL WAR SAGAS

BESTSELLING ROMANCES BY JANELLE TAYLOR

SAVAGE ECSTASY (824, $3.50)

It was like lightning striking, the first time the Indian brave Gray Eagle looked into the eyes of the beautiful young settler Alisha. And from the moment he saw her, he knew that he must possess her — and make her his slave!

DEFIANT ECSTASY (931, $3.50)

When Gray Eagle returned to Fort Pierre's gates with his hundred warriors behind him, Alisha's heart skipped a beat: would Gray Eagle destroy her — or make his destiny her own?

FORBIDDEN ECSTASY (1014, $3.50)

Gray Eagle had promised Alisha his heart forever — nothing could keep him from her. But when Alisha woke to find her red-skinned lover gone, she felt abandoned and alone. Lost between two worlds, desperate and fearful of betrayal, Alisha hungered for the return of her FORBIDDEN ECSTASY.

Available wherever paperbacks are sold, or order direct from the Publisher. Send cover price plus 50¢ per copy for mailing and handling to Zebra Books, 475 Park Avenue South, New York, N.Y. 10016. DO NOT SEND CASH.

READ THESE PAGE-TURNING ROMANCES!